AB

ABOUT THE LAST VAN LARSEN/
PLOTKIN NOVEL

FIRST PUBLICATION ANYWHERE!

By George Baxt:

GEORGE BAXT

SATAN IS A WOMAN

A CRIME CLASSIC®

INTERNATIONAL POLYGONICS, LTD.
NEW YORK CITY

Any similarity to persons living or dead is unintended and purely coincidental. Locations, Astoroth House and the Old Avon, etc., are also the products of the author's imagination.

SATAN IS A WOMAN
First publication.

Library of Congress Card Catalog No. 87-82450
ISBN 0-930330-65-X

Printed and manufactured in the United States of America by Guinn Printing, New York.
First IPL printing October 1987.
10 9 8 7 6 5 4 3 2 1

This book is for
Barbara Shelley
and
Clive Hirshhorn

CHAPTER
one

Sylvia Plotkin, shining like a good deed in a naughty world, emerged from the jumbo jet.

"Hello, London!" she trilled in a burst of infectious enthusiasm, and the stewardess at the foot of the stairs rewarded her with a smile that would remain nailed to her face until the last first class passenger had disembarked.

"Mind your step!" cautioned the stewardess. Sylvia clutched the handrail with her right hand and her breast with her left.

"England at last!" she caroled over her shoulder to her traveling companion, Edna St. Thomas Shelley. "England! Shakespeare! Browning! Kippers! Elizabeths one and two!"

"Albert Finney," chorused Edna with hungry relish as she gave one last epicurean look to the purser who favored her with an appreciative wink. "Move, Sylvia, you're holding up the line."

"Urmph," gasped the purser and Edna withdrew two delinquent fingers.

"We're at the Dorchester," whispered Edna and the purser's cheeks flushed.

7

"Heavens!" cried Sylvia as she paused halfway down, "what's with the thundering herd?" Heading towards the jet across the tarmac were a dozen men and women, a fourth of whom were brandishing cameras, followed by a van bearing a portable television camera.

The stewardess clasped her fingers together like an arthritic nun abandoning her beads. "Aren't you Sylvia Plotkin, the celebrated American authoress?"

Sylvia lowered her eyes demurely and spoke with an alien modesty. "Why, yes, my latest, *I Am Curious (Jewish)*, my autobiography, is in its thirty-eighth week on the *New York Times* best seller list, having merely slipped to second position."

"You forgot your name, rank, and serial number," snapped Edna as she fumbled in her purse, found a powder puff, and attacked her face with it mercilessly.

The stewardess rushed up and took Sylvia's hand and guided her down the remaining stairs to one side. Edna, with a graceful wave of a hand, spurred the press towards their quarry.

"*This* is Miss Plotkin and *I* am Edna St. Thomas Shelley, her editor, friend, and confidante, in no particular order, and we are perfectly *thrilled* to be in England . . . "

She was rudely jostled aside in mid-sentence as the first photographers angled at Sylvia.

"Smile, Sylvia!" directed the undaunted Edna.

"Urmph!" cried a photographer who had innocently positioned himself in Edna's line of fire.

The television truck screeched to a halt and a photographer leapt out of the van and clambered behind the camera. The sound man elbowed his way towards Sylvia with a portable microphone, the interviewer trailing him with the solemn look of a nanny in search of a nursery.

Sylvia revelled in the unexpected homage. "Ladies and Gentlemen, I'm *overwhelmed*!" she gurgled. Questions flew at her like a barrage of tennis balls, and she returned each serve like a professional.

"How old are you, Miss Plotkin?"

"Not old enough for Medicare and still young enough to take the pill."

"Who's your favorite English author?"

"Agatha Christie."

"Who's your favorite English actress?"

"Coral Browne."

"Who's your favorite English comedian?"

"Prince Andrew."

"What do you think of the Tory government.?"

"They're a bit conservative."

"Have you completely abandoned your vocation as a school teacher?"

"I am on a year's sabbatical from Robert F. Wagner High School in New York City."

"Much to the children's relief," added Edna in an acid-tinged aside.

"What are your views of the American political scene?"

"Myopic."

For a few moments, Sylvia bathed merrily in the wave of laughter that engulfed her. Edna examined a finger-nail and the television cameraman.

A sharp-faced female reporter with the determined look of a wasp in heat and vocal chords freshly sand-papered quickly interjected. "Isn't American society growing a bit incestuous?"

Riposted Sylvia, "What's a little incest as long as you keep it in the family?" and then privately wondered what's been going on at home they've been keeping from her.

"What about Max Van Larsen?"

Sylvia froze. She felt a soft, feminine hand take hers and squeeze it gently, and realized with gratitude it was Edna. Sylvia's eyes sought the source of the interroga-tion and divined it was the young man on her left with

9

thinning blond hair, laser-beam blue eyes, and a nose that pointed forward like an accusing finger.

"What about Max Van Larsen?" he repeated.

"Did you meet him when he was here?" asked Sylvia in a voice that needed oiling.

The young man nodded curtly. "I interviewed him briefly. I was to see him again for lunch a week ago Saturday, but I gather he took ill rather suddenly and returned to America in the company of two male nurses."

"They were adorable," chimed in Edna as she tightened her grip on Sylvia's hand, "I believe they were in crew for Oxford." Her eyes took on a slight glaze. "They still have remarkable strokes."

A train wreck couldn't sidetrack the reporter. "They told me here at Heathrow that he was taken aboard the plane in a straitjacket."

"Something he bought at Harrod's," snapped Edna.

"Please, Edna. The gentleman is directing his questions at me." Sylvia drew herself up to her full five foot four and pulled her hand away from Edna's in a movement as brave and majestic as Joan of Arc lighting her own funeral pyre. "Yes, Mr. Van Larsen returned to New York a bit under the weather. He has been under a severe strain." She managed a hollow chuckle. "I assume, every so often, even Atlas sagged."

"And he's still in a sanatorium?"

"Well he's certainly not at Grossinger's," countered Sylvia sweetly. "Max Van Larsen is the greatest detective in New York City's Bureau of Missing Persons. He will most certainly find himself."

"I believe you and Mr. Van Larsen are considered, shall we say, engaged?"

"We've managed to keep ourselves busy the past two years."

"Yet you left him to come here to exploit your lastest book."

"Well, actually," began Sylvia, with what she hoped was a touch of levity," the doctors suggested my absence might speed his recovery. There was a certain to-do about my insisting he be put on a diet of chicken soup and . . . well . . . they had to replace the bars on his window."

"Could some of the severe strain he's been under possibly be attributed to Lady Valerie Crawford?"

From the look on Sylvia's face she might have just been dealt a straight flush. "Lady Valerie Crawford? You mean the actress, Lady Valerie Crawford?"

"I believe Mr. Van Larsen spent a great deal of time with her."

(A stern admonition received ten hours earlier returned to Sylvia's memory. *"Beware the British Press*, Sylvia. They're tough, they're tenacious, and they dig for dirt. Keep on your toes.")

"Get off your toes," said Edna out of the side of her ample mouth, "you look like a Harlem Globetrotter."

Sylvia had the bewildered feeling of a rabid Zionist who just discovered she'd been adopted from an Arab orphanage. Pull yourself together, Plotkin, she said to herself. The worst is yet to come. Have you ever thought for one moment Max was completely faithful? What man in your life—beginning with that rat of an ex-husband, Isaac—has ever been completely faithful? And what is completely faithful? Total paralysis is completely faithful.

"I'm sure had Mr. Van Larsen been lucid," said Sylvia staunchly, "he would have dropped the lady's name in the course of conversation. In his present condition, I think we are safe in assuming he has dropped the lady."

Edna smiled with pride. Plotkin was back in control.

The television interviewer came to Sylvia's rescue. He spoke with a sexy suavity that could have sold her cigars. "What is the subject of the next book, Miss Plotkin?"

"Witchcraft," replied Sylvia swiftly. She thought somewhere to her left she heard a deep intake of breath.

"Ah!" said the television interviewer as though holding a snifter of brandy under his nose. "How fascinating! You're aware the practice is on the uprise here?"

"I most certainly am. I gather the country's crawling with covens. Actually," she continued, wrinkling her nose with a coy winsomeness, "I've become a bit of a dabbler in the black arts myself lately."

"Not really!"

"Oh *yes*! Double, double, toil, and trouble, eye of newt, and all that jazz. In fact, Miss Shelley and I are charter members of the E.H.D.O.S."

"The E.H.D.O.S.?"

"The East Hampton Daughters of Satan. Aren't we, Edna dear?"

"Oh, we most certainly are, dear," Edna duetted slightly off-key, "in fact I've got the broomstick concession, ha, ha, ha."

The laser-beam-eyed reporter positioned himself in front of Sylvia again. "That makes two things you have in common with Lady Valerie. She's quite a sorceress."

"Well actually, I'm only an apprentice sorceress, but I'm always willing to learn a new trick. Do you know Lady Valerie personally?"

"Oh yes. I was at Eton with her son."

Her son. Relief flooded Sylvia's soul and was reflected in her face. *Son.* She must be fifty at *least.*

"Perhaps you could arrange for me to meet her. We're at the Dorchester. What's your name?"

"Nick Hastings." He smiled slightly. "Valerie's in rehearsal at the moment, the new version of *Hamlet* being done at the Old Avon."

"*No!*" expostulated Sylvia. "What a *coincidence!* If you've read my autobiography, then you certainly understand the coincidence! Our dear, darling, beloved Madame Vilna's *directing* it! It's her adaptation! She was invited here especially by the Old Avon Company to stage it!" She turned to the other members of the press. "Madame Vilna, for those of you who have *not* read my autobiography, was a major character in two of the big cases in which Mr. Van Larsen and I were involved, and she's waiting to hear from me right now." Her eyes found Nick Hastings again. "Can you imagine? Madame Vilna directing the aforementioned Lady Valerie Crawford. What part is she playing?"

"Ophelia, of course."

"Of course. Leave it to Vilna," said Sylvia with a wicked grin, "she can teach an old dog new tricks."

Out of the corner of her eye, Edna watched the last two passengers leaving the jet, one a tall priest wearing thick horn-rimmed glasses and his hat pulled tight down to his ears, leading a smaller, much younger priest who appeared to have a hump on his back. The stewardness overheard the elder priest inquire of his companion, "By the way, I've been meaning to ask you, who was that laity I saw you with last night?"

The sharp-faced female reporter who identified herself as Evelyn Blair now held the inquisitory spotlight.

"Miss Plotkin, you wouldn't by any chance be in London to continue the job Max Van Larsen left unfinished?"

"Well actually, Miss Blair, Joseph Gordon, who sent for Max when his daughter Lisa disappeared, *is* an old friend. In fact, I expected him to meet our plane."

The stewardess interjected, "He's sent a car and chauffeur."

"Oh, how thoughtful," said Sylvia with an appropriate smile. "Did you hear that, Edna. Joe's sent a car."

"And chauffeur," added Edna eagerly, anxious to examine the specimen.

"Miss Plotkin," said Miss Blair with an exaggerated patience, "you haven't answered my question."

"Ah yes . . . well . . . let me put it this way, Miss Blair, should my assistance be requested by Mr. Gordon, he

13

will receive it. I never turn my back on a friend."

Nick Hastings spoke again. " I assume you're aware that at the time of her disappearance, Lisa Gordon was researching a projected book on witchcraft?"

"I most certainly do," said Sylvia sternly, "she was in my employ,—my leg-woman, so to speak. I assure you this trip to London wasn't on the spur of the moment. It was planned months ago when Madame Vilna received her offer from the Old Avon. Max's S.O.S. from Joe Gordon was, of course, coincidental. Poor Lisa's disappearance! I've been praying for her safe deliverance."

"Praying to Satan?" inquired Evelyn Blair.

"No, dear," replied Sylvia blandly, "in special cases I patronize my local synagogue."

Edna restrained an impulse to pat Sylvia on the head.

The building housing the Old Avon Shakespearian Company was a newly constucted edifice on the banks of the Thames in central London, a short distance from the imposing Royal Festival Hall. In addition to the large semi-circular auditorium and dressing rooms, it contained an excellent restaurant and numerous small bars on its three interior levels. Inside the auditorium, the day's rehearsal of Madame Vilna's adaptation of *Hamlet* was about to get underway. Over three dozen actors were milling about the stage in various degrees of expectancy, eagerness, and impatience awaiting the arrival of their director, Madame Vilna.

In the stage doorkeeper's glass-enclosed office, Lady Valerie Crawford held the telephone to her ear. She was a handsome woman whose Jean Muir trouser suit added stature to her medium height. Her hair and complexion were a matching blond, and the natural eyelashes that protected her green-brown eyes jutted stiffly like porcupine quills. The doorkeeper sitting behind his desk had a neutral expression on his face as he doped the greyhound races from his form sheet. Neither he nor Lady Valerie were aware of a young man who had come slouching through the stage door and positioned himself in the doorway to the office, sipping black coffee from a plastic container.

Dylan Wake's bloodshot eyes were heavy with hangover. His shaggy red hair hung past his ears like a mass of uncarded wool. His skin was drawn tautly about his face with tiny telltale blue veins around the nose and eyes which somehow never seemed to lose their Irish twinkle. He wore his standard uniform of blue jeans, a yellow cotton shirt, and frayed leather jacket. Under his right arm he held in a viselike grip a wellthumbed script of *Hamlet.* He was in his late twenties but looked older. Dylan's height was an inch short of six feet but his chronic slouch made him seem shorter. If he was eavesdropping deliberately, there was no strain on his ears. Lady Valerie's decibel rating always held at the danger level.

"You darling lad," she trumpeted into the phone, causing the doorkeeper to wince," how kind of you to phone and tell me. I will see you this weekend, won't I?" *I* rising like the top note of an air raid siren. "Oh goody, goody, good. What was that Nicky?" As she listened solemnly to the voice at the other end of the phone, her lips parted in a wry smile. "We'll simply have to exercise patience until further developments, won't we?" I have to dash now darling. Rehearsal, you know. That Vilna woman's an absolute martinet. I'll speak to you later. Bless you for *everything.*"

As she replaced the phone, her face a study, Dylan Wake lowered the coffee container from his lips and spoke. "And how is dear Nicky today, me old darlin'?"

Lady Valerie turned and smiled artificially in recognition, "Nicky's just fine." Then she folded her arms as her voice darkened. "Where did you disappear to last night?"

"Last night? Last night?" He was examining the ceiling. "Now, what was last night?"

"You know bloody well what was with last night. You were to join my supper party at the Buxton," emphasizing the name as though by some momentary attack of amnesia he might have forgotten the actor's club, one of many that proliferated in London's West End.

"I loathe the place," he said with unmasked distaste. "Actors only meet there to compare poverty."

"Where were you?"

"With Nelly Locke."

Her pupils dilated with astonishment. "I thought you'd written finish to that story."

"So last night I decided to add a postscript," he said with a shrug. He tossed the empty container into a wastepaper basket. "We were going over our lines."

"I don't know what possessed that Vilna woman, appointing Nelly my understudy. If only her talent matched her ambition. I think she's absolutely hopeless."

"She was fine last night," said Dylan with a pixieish grin. "She helped me find a new dimension in Laertes."

"What with?"

"Now don't be vulgar."

Stonily, she walked briskly past him into the gangway toward the stage. Dylan chuckled and spoke to the old man behind the desk. "Well, Paddy me ol' darlin', what looks promising at White City tonight?"

"Witches' Brew in the third," the doorkeeper rasped without looking up.

"Witches' Brew." Dylan fumbled in his jacket pocket and found a ten-shilling coin and flipped it onto the desk. "Place that for me, will you, me old love?" The old man nodded as the actor slouched away.

Jingle jangle jingle jangle

The bells at the end of the pendant earrings were attached to the earlobes of a stunning, imposing woman whose two hundred pounds were extremely well distributed. Her jet black hair (through the courtesy of Elizabeth Arden) was pulled back tightly in a bun held in place by two red Spanish combs. As she advanced with Gulliver strides down the center aisle of the auditorium towards the stage, her purple velvet cape billowed like an uprooted canvas tent at the mercy of a hurricane. Under the cape she wore a yellow lace-trimmed blouse with a red dickey, and her legs were encased in specially designed orange sailor pants. From her left arm swung a huge black carpetbag.

She opened her mouth and broke the sound barrier. "Vilna approaches!"

All conversation ceased onstage.

"Vilna apologizes for her tardiness but there was the inevitable changing of the guard outside Buckingham Palace, which delayed the progress of my extremely antiquated taxi cab! Good morning! Good morning! Are we all bright-eyed, bushy-tailed, and ready to attack our *Hamlet* from the right flank?" She pronounced, "Hamlet" "omelet". Briskly flinging her carpetbag onto the aisle seat of the first row, she climbed the makeshift wooden steps leading to the stage, and with hands on her hips, surveyed her company of actors.

"Is everybody present and accounted for?" she bellowed and was answered with a chorus of assent.

"How's me old darlin' this morning?" shouted Dylan as he wearily followed Lady Valerie on stage.

Madame Vilna fixed him with an icy eye. "Vilna is at the top of her form, you *shikker.*"

"That means 'drunkard,' " one actor whispered to another.

Vilna clapped two beefy hands together. "All right! All right! Sirs on the right side of the stage, Dames on the left side, and upstage center will group the ordinary actors to whom, of course, I am most partial." She embellished the last part of her statement with a smile that could have baked bread. Vilna watched as the actors slowly separated into her designated groups.

Dames, Vilna thought to herself, *Sirs.* Overaged but still spirited like herself. Resentful of this foreign intruder from the colonies, but still affording her a grudging respect. Yet inwardly, she knew they raged at her bizarre, outlandish, yet provocatively challenging new interpretation of the Bard's masterpiece. Vilna was invigorated by this new experience, basking in the pride of being invited to direct one of England's most honored and revered acting companies. To her, this was like bathing in the fountain of youth. She felt like a young girl again, although she had made her debut easily half a century ago with the Moshe Rabinowitz Funambulists in Moscow.

Weeks earlier, she had described the occasion with total recall to Dylan Wake, to whom she had immediately become partial. "I was but a mere child at the time," she told Dylan over tea at Fortnam and Mason, the young rake immediately mesmerized by the woman's recital. "Rabinowitz spotted me in the chorus line of the Odessa Operetta Theatre during a performance of *Zie Hutt Tsoofill Gelt,* which is perhaps more familiar to you as *The Merry Widow.* He presented himself to me backstage, invited me to supper, which of course I accepted with alacrity, and took me to a private room at the Alte Katchke, which is the equivalent of your White Elephant restaurant here. He told me that when I first kicked my leg up he recognized my potential, told me if I would work hard and obey him implicitly I would be a star, and when I agreed to place my future in his most seductive hands, "she slapped her thigh and let out
deflower me
ap-

An old lady at the next table had closed her eyes, emitted a groan, and fainted with her head falling face down into a slice of strawberry cream pie, but neither Vilna nor Dylan had noticed. Under the table, Dylan's hand had strayed to Vilna's knee and the old woman wagged a beefy finger under his nose. "The gesture is flattering but unappreciated, buddy boy." He had removed his hand with his stock impish grin as she continued, "From our few rehearsals, I have seen traces in you of what Rabinowitz first saw in me, way back there in the dark ages. But I was *dedicated*. I am still dedicated. You are not dedicated. You could be a great actor, Dylan. A very great actor. But you dissipate yourself. Sometimes when I look at you, it is as though you are in a trance . . . *bewitched!*"

Bewitched.

Madame Vilna shook herself free of her reverie and studied the three groups of her company. She cleared her throat. "Before I begin the exercises that will relax our bodies and our voices, I wish to explain a certain preoccupation you may have detected in Vilna the past two weeks. I have been most concerned with the well being of my dear friend, Max Van Larsen, whom several of you have come to know personally through my good auspices," her eyes darting rapidly from Dylan to Lady Valerie to Nelly Locke and Dame Augusta Mayhew, an octogenerian Vilna had selected for the role of the Player Queen.

"Last night I spoke to a mutual friend in New York who, God willing, should at this very moment be arriving at your Heathrow Airport, and her news of Max was most encouraging. *Most* encouraging."

Lady Valerie's fingers were admonishing a stray hair. "I now assure you," Madame Vilna continued as her eyes fixed on the diminutive Nelly Locke (whose hands

19

though held stiffly at her sides appeared to be trembling),
"I most assuredly assure you that our rehearsals will continue full speed ahead with confidence and mutual
respect, and will give London a *Hamlet* . . . " raising her
right hand with the index finger pointing to the roof, "it
will not soon forget!"

"Amen," said Dame Augusta Mayhew in a voice that
had traveled from the lower regions of her abdomen.

"Now then!" boomed Madame Vilna, "Our first exercise! Line up! Face each other!" She dug into her trouser
pockets, extracted a pitch pipe, raised it to her lips, exhaled, and the entire company sang:

"How do you do my partnerrrrrr

How do you do to-dayyyyyy"

Madame Vilna nodded her head in tempo, using her
right hand as a baton, stamping her right foot as a
metronome, and privately wondering if her beloved
Sylvia Plotkin would survive this visit to London.

CHAPTER
two

Gurgling merrily like one of the fountains in Trafalgar Square, Edna St. Thomas Shelley settled comfortably next to Sylvia Plotkin in the back seat of the Rolls Royce. She turned her head and through the rear window watched the young chauffeur placing their luggage in the boot. The gurgle abated as Edna vocally stamped the young man with her seal of approval, "He's beautiful."

"You're overdoing the man-eater bit, Edna," admonished Sylvia as she wiped her perspiring brow with a tissue.

"Believe me, Sylvia, a thing of beauty is a goy forever." Edna turned to Sylvia. "I think we both did beautifully."

"I didn't push the witchcraft bit too hard?"

"You were subtler then a French perfume."

"I think we struck paydirt. Particularly that Nick Hastings. If he wasn't so young, I'd say he trained with the Gestapo."

"That Evelyn Blair person comes in a close second." She mimicked the reporter viciously. " 'Praying to Satan?' " Self-satisfaction settled smugly over Edna's attractive face. "Not bad for starters, not bad at all. You were gorgeous with the Lady Valerie bit."

Sylvia drummed two fingers on her right knee. "Imagine a woman her age playing Ophelia! Still," she added with a sigh, "Bernhardt played L'Aiglon on one leg when she was sixty."

They heard the boot slammed shut. The chauffeur crossed to the left side of the Rolls Royce, opened the door, placed two hat boxes on the seat, smiled amiably at his two passengers, shut the door, and headed around the front of the vehicle towards the right side.

"Good teeth," commented Edna.

"Where?"

"The chauffeur. I always thought the British had bad teeth."

"I guess there's been an improvement since National Health." Sylvia lowered her head conspiratorially. "Careful what you say. No telling who he is." Edna nodded. The chauffeur slid behind the steering wheel, shut the door, turned the ignition key, revved the powerful motor, shifted into gear, and nosed towards London as Edna studied a prominent red birthmark under his right ear.

As he carefully maneuvered away from the airport traffic, Sylvia engaged him in conversation. "What's your name, dear?" It might have been the first day of the autumn semester at Robert F. Wagner High School. Edna chose the interval to refresh her makeup.

"Harry, miss," said the chauffeur genially, a trace of the Midlands in his accent, "Harry Sanders."

"Have you been with Mr. Gordon a long time?"

"About six months, miss."

"I must say," said Sylvia, gently nudging Edna with her knee, "foreign correspondents certainly do all right for themselves. A Rolls Royce and chauffeur!"

"The car's on hire, miss." Edna studied his face in the rearview mirror. "Special for this occasion."

"How sweet of Joe! Isn't that sweet of Joe, Edna?"

"I could cry."

"Actually," continued Harry the chauffeur, "I'm sort of Mr. Gordon's private secretary. He's a very decent bloke, Mr. Gordon. The only person to give me a job after I got out of the nick."

Nick, thought Edna. Too coincidental. Nick Hastings. Old Nick, one of Satan's many aliases.

"Nick?" repeated Sylvia as though reading Edna's mind.

Harry grinned. "Jail. The pokey. English slang."

Edna was fascinated. "What were you in for?"

"Assault with attempt to kill," he replied matter-of-factly. "I got two years that time."

Harry chuckled. "The nick's my home away from home." Sylvia's fingers nervously formed a cat's cradle. Edna, arms folded, was hypnotized. "Served three years in Borstal when I was just a kid of twelve. Beat my old man over the head with a length of pipe. Nasty old bugger, the old man. He threw one punch too many at my mum, so I let him have it." He beeped his car at a red Volvo attempting to cut in front of him. Sylvia stared out the window and saw Nick Hastings at the wheel, Evelyn Blair at his side, her mouth moving with the rapidity of a shuttlecock. Sylvia nudged Edna. Edna had already seen. Harry maneuvered the Rolls into the outside lane.

"Tried to go straight when I got out of Borstal," they heard Harry saying imperviously, "but got in with a bad lot in Chelsea. Did a year for burglary, then another two years for peddling hash . . . was forced into that bit but the fuzz wouldn't believe a two-time loser . . . not old Harry . . ."

Old Harry, thought Sylvia, this is too much. Nick, now Old Harry, another alias for the Devil.

"Then came the assault with attempt to kill rap. Some bleeding actor was responsible for that one." Edna recognized his use of "bleeding" in its derogatory sense. "Had a fight in a pub over some bint."

"I beg your pardon?" That came from Sylvia.

23

Harry smiled. "Bint ... girl ... whore ... all the same."

"What quaint slang you have in this country," commented Sylvia.

"Well, anyway," breezed on Harry, "I got the redheaded bastard out in the street, punched him a stiff one in the belly, and when he fell to the pavement, I stomped his head just to teach him."

Sylvia scratched her cheek with a fingertip. "I hope he was a good pupil."

"Oh, he learnt all right. Two years for that one. That was my last rap. My parole officer got me to Mr. Gordon and thanks to him, I've sort of found religion and reformed." He stared out his right window at the red Volvo which had caught up with them. "If that sonofabitch tries to cut me off again, I'll run him in the side and do him."

"Now, now," cautioned Edna with a twinkle in her voice, "we'd hate to lose you to the authorities again."

"He's a bloody fool. That Volvo's no match for this tank."

In a sudden burst of speed, the Volvo shot forward and disappeared into traffic.

"I suppose you know Lisa Gordon?" asked Sylvia.

"Sure. Poor kid. Four weeks now she's missing. Mr. Gordon fought like hell to keep it out of the papers."

(*"Miss Plotkin, you wouldn't by any chance be in London to continue the job Max Van Larsen left unfinished?"* Evelyn Blair's voice was as sandpaper clear in Sylvia's mind as though she were seated next to Harry repeating the question.)

"The reporters at the airport seemed to know all about it," said Sylvia.

"Oh, they all know, but they've been asked not to use it. Not yet."

"When was the last time you saw her?" asked Edna with the subtlety of a nudge in the ribs.

24

"Four weeks ago, when I drove her to Astoroth House for the weekend."

"Astoroth House?" asked Sylvia.

"You must have heard of Astoroth House!" Harry exclaimed. "It used to be one of our biggest tourist attractions until it was closed to the public about a year ago. Dame Augusta Mayhew's place."

"Why, of course," admonished Edna as she turned to Sylvia, "it goes back to the Ancient Order of Druids founded in England in seventeen hundred and eighty-one."

"Much earlier than that," corrected Harry, "it was built by the first Mayhew, Hugo the Hairy, in the early fifteenth century after getting a royal grant. He was the king's torturer you know. The stuff's still there."

"What stuff?" asked Edna.

"Hugo's torture stuff. It's in the subterranean cellar. Soundproof so you couldn't hear his victims screaming. Seen it myself. It's super." He said "super" with a lascivious relish that sent a chill down Sylvia's spine. "Then in the sixteen hundreds, it was a hotbed of practice of the black arts." A professional tour guide couldn't have been more erudite or articulate. Sylvia had the feeling that what Harry was telling them might have been committed to memory. "That was the time of Sir Martin Mayhew, surely you've heard of him, Marty the Malicious? They burned *him* at the stake along with his wife, Agnes the Asinine. Reputed to be a big blabbermouth which is what done old Marty in. Their kids were spared of course, which is how come the line survived right down to Dame Augusta Mayhew's late husband, Irving. He passed on three years ago."

"What was Lisa's connection with Astoroth House?"

"Over on your right, ladies, that's Hogarth's House." Edna and Sylvia dutifully glanced out the window and then Sylvia repeated the question.

"Well, I suppose I'm not talking out of turn. It's nothing Mr. Gordon won't tell you himself. We're more like mates than employer and hired hand, him and me. She was doing some investigating into witchcraft."

"Yes, I know," said Sylvia evenly. "She was doing it for me. I'm a celebrated American authoress and my next book deals with the black arts."

"Hey! You must be Mr. Van Larsen's gal!"

"Yes," said Sylvia with the pride of Michaelangelo lying back to examine his progress on the Sistine Chapel, "I'm his bint."

Harry erupted with laughter and then swiftly turned the wheel to avoid an undesired marriage with an oil truck. Unruffled he inquired, "How is he? Real decent bloke, Mr. Van Larsen."

"He's coming along," said Sylvia. Edna rubbed the tip of her nose.

"Well, anyway," continued the chauffeur blithely, "seems there's been quite a bit of going on up at Astoroth House since it was closed to the public."

"Witchcraft?" Sylvia tolled the word.

"The Order of the Fallen Angels."

"How quaint," commented Edna drily.

"It's no secret," said Harry, "it's been written up. It's Lady Valerie Crawford's bunch." Edna patted Sylvia's hand. "She's one of the high priestesses."

"Heavens," said Sylvia, "when does she find the time? She's so busy rehearsing with the Old Avon."

"So's Dame Augusta. She's Valerie's aunt. Lady Valerie's married to Dame August's nephew, Sir Vernon Mayhew."

"Lady Valerie's *married*?" Sylvia was leaning forward now, her hands clutching the back of the front seat.

"Let me put it this way. She's had no reason to divorce him. Not even after the scandal."

"*What* scandal?" It was Edna's turn to lean forward.

"Around five years ago. Old Vernon used to be a famous

doctor. Then there was some kadiddle about malpractice and he was stricken off the rolls. It cost the family plenty to get it hushed up and keep him out of the nick. Turned out the old sod was an illegal abortionist."

"How sad for the sod," said Sylvia.

"He lives up at Astoroth House. Spends his time looking after the zoo."

"Oh, is there a zoo near Astoroth House?" Sylvia inquired innocently.

"They have a private zoo. It used to be one of the big attractions for the kids."

"Heavens to Betsy," caroled Edna, "it must take quite a bit of money for the upkeep."

"They seem to manage."

The thirty-second silence that ensued was broken by Sylvia. "You dropped Lisa at Astoroth House and returned to London?"

"Yes, miss."

"And she was never seen again?"

"I took her up Friday afternoon and then came back to London. It's only an hour's drive. Then Lisa phoned her father late that night and whatever she told him must have upset him terribly, because he got me at my digs around two in the morning and asked me to drive him up to the place. Well, by the time I got dressed, picked him up, and got to the old house, it was sunrise. Lady Valerie took Mr. Gordon to Lisa's room but the bed hadn't been slept in. Lisa was gone, along with her overnight case and her belongings. Lady Valerie was very upset."

"And what upset Lisa?" Sylvia rubbed her damp palms together.

"I don't know. I never learned. Mr. Gordon kept it to himself until he sent for Mr. Van Larsen."

I have my work cut out for me, thought Sylvia as her fingertips began to tingle in anticipation.

"What about the other guests," Sylvia heard Edna inquire. "Couldn't they offer any possible explanation for Lisa's mysterious defection?"

"Guess they couldn't, miss. We were there for at least five hours while Mr. Gordon made local inquiries. You know, the village cab service, train station, bus station, the works. Nobody'd seen a pretty nineteen-year-old girl with an overnight case. Anyway, we came back to London and Mr. Gordon put some private detectives on the case, but they weren't getting any results, so he sent for Mr. Van Larsen. It was me that drove him to Astoroth House *that* weekend."

"Oh?"

"And it was me what drove him back on Sunday . . . raving mad." Sylvia struggled to keep from trembling. "Mr. Gordon and that bastard Dylan Wake were in the back seat holding him down."

"Mr. Gordon was there for the weekend, too?" asked Edna with a tinge of surprise.

"Well, he's a great friend of Lady Valerie and her aunt. It wasn't their fault Lisa suddenly upped and disappeared. She's a strange kid, always doing things on impulse. Boy, did Van Larsen fight. It took the other one to belt him on the chin and flatten him unconscious."

"The other one?" Sylvia's face had the perplexed look of a beaver who'd bitten into a floating log only to discover in chagrin that the log was an alligator. "What other one?"

"The wild American lady."

"We have loads of those," said Edna archly.

"Madame Vilna, I think her name was."

Sylvia felt the blood draining from her face as Edna clutched her hand.

"Madame Vilna happens to be a friend of ours," contributed Edna. "We didn't know she'd been with Max that weekend. Max forgot to tell us." Sylvia kicked her gently.

"Vilna certainly has a great deal to tell us, doesn't she,

Edna." Sylvia's voice was flatter than a heliport. "What was that other name you mentioned?"

"Dylan Wake?" His voice might have been rubbed with ashes.

"Yes, that's it. Who's he?"

"The redheaded bastard's an actor with the Old Avon."

"Ah!" exclaimed Sylvia. "I suppose that explains his presence at Astoroth House that weekend."

"I think he's been having it off with Lady Valerie," informed Harry.

"Having it off?" Sylvia was making a mental note to purchase a dictionary of British slang if any such animal was in print.

Harry's birthmark seemed to glow as he explained with embarrassment. "You know . . . doing her."

Edna smile with benevolence. "You mean sleeping with her, dear."

Harry's voice grew harder. "He'll sleep with anything as long as it breathes and isn't nailed down. He's the reason for my last stretch in the nick. He's the one I stomped."

Sylvia's palms were damp again. "It must have been rather awkward meeting him again."

"That wasn't the first time we'd met since I got out. He and Lady Valerie see a lot of Mr. Gordon. Dylan's an arrogant little bastard. 'And how's me old darlin' he asked the first time we met after Mr. Gordon hired me. Easy as that, see. Oozing his phoney Irish charm, like two years out of my life was nothing to him."

"The brains spilling from his head wouldn't have been pleasant either," cautioned Edna.

Harry drove in silence until they reached the Hammersmith bypass, a stretch of elevated road over the London suburb.

"Where are we?" asked Sylvia.

"We're coming over Hammersmith. This takes us into

Cromwell Road, in another ten minutes we'll be at the Dorchester."

"It's charming."

Edna crossed her legs. "How's Mr. Gordon been taking all this? His daughter disappears, then his best friend comes over to help and ends up off his rocker. Ouch." Sylvia had kicked her again.

"He's a real stoic, Mr. Gordon. He's one bloke who knows how to roll with the punches. He knows Mr. Van Larsen is in good hands and he's *positive* he'll find Lisa. Scotland Yard's hard at it."

Sylvia spoke slowly. "And what does Mr. Gordon think of the Order of Fallen Angels?"

Edna admired the muscles beneath the uniform as Harry shrugged.

"There's a lot of that sort of stuff going on these days. Mr. Gordon says it's all over the place. Takes people's minds off the rotten state the world is in. but that Madame Vilna! Blimey! She had a lot to say about it— and none of it pleasant. Quite a bird, that old lady."

"Oh yes," said Sylvia through a smile, "she's quite a bird. In fact, in our immediate circle she's considered a delicacy."

"Wouldn't it be fascinating," giggled Sylvia, "if *we* got caught up in local occult circles?"

"Yes, wouldn't it," replied Edna, "but then, I suppose it's more fun than basket weaving."

Nelly Locke sat with Dame Augusta Mayhew in the rear of the auditorium watching Vilna's frantic rehearsal. A knitting bag rested on Dame Augusta's fragile lap and her nimble fingers belied their age as needles and wool rapidly increased the size of the work in progress, a thick scarf.

"Penny for them," she whispered to the preoccupied young understudy.

"Ohhh," replied Nelly with a drawn-out sigh, "I was just wondering when I'll see my name in lights."

"When you change it," said the older woman huskily.

Nelly turned and stared at her. "To what?"

"Exit."

Click click click.

Nelly clenched her teeth and re-directed her eyes to the stage as she heard Vilna cry, "That will not do at alllll, Lady Valerie, not at alllll!"

"I feel *quite* comfortable with what I'm doing," countered Lady Valerie, throwing down an invisible gauntlet. Vilna's hands made delicate circles in the air and then gently alighted on each hip. The company collectively held its breath as Vilna moved slowly towards Lady Valerie and Dylan Wake, like a cat espying two innocent pigeons and revelling in the abundance of the menu.

"Valiant Valerie," purred Vilna, "when Ophelia enters, she must waft upon the stage like a nimbus gently buffeted by a spring breeze," her voice rose an octave and sounded like a tuba attempting 'The Flight Of The Bumble Bee,' " she must *not* enter like a bull elephant sniffing for peanuts!"

Lady Valerie's cheeks reddened and her eyes narrowed as she heard Dylan cackling under his breath. Madame Vilna was now stationed in the wings.

"Watch *me*!" Vilna bellowed. Gently, daintily, she lifted her hands, cocking her head to one side like an anxious swallow seeking directions to Capistrano, and then, with a half skip and an astonishing grace that belied her weight and her years, made her entrance.

"She's beautiful," whispered Dylan. Lady Valerie's unladylike reply almost cause him to wince.

"That is how Ophelia must enter!" Vilna had stomped center stage. "You must keep this in mind, Lady Valerie. Forget what Shakespeare wrote. There were no out-of-town tryouts in his day. Had such existed then, much would have been altered, and I have altered as though there was an out-of-town tryout. How often must I repeat? *My* Ophelia is a nymphomaniac! You must keep in mind she has slept with half of Elsinore, give or take a smidgin!"

"Impossible!" shouted Lady Valerie.

"Positively!" thundered Vilna. "She has scored with everybody *except* Hamlet and suspects he is impotent—if not sleeping with her beloved brother, Laertes," pointing a finger at Dylan who was smirking. "There! There stands your Hamlet. Look at him!"

All eyes were on the venerable Sir Leonard Greystoke, who at the age of sixty-three looked thirty years younger, thanks to a recent three-month stay at the celebrated Swiss Institute of Rejuvenation. "Is that not a monument of impotence?"

Sir Leonard stiffened. "Now see here, my good woman!"

Vilna beamed coquettishly. "Of course, only within the context of this interpretation, Sir Leonard, darling bubbeleh. It goes without saying you are a symbol of sex of many decades standing, but, nevertheless, you must inspire Lady Valerie with this deception or else she will be entering and exiting for the rest of the afternoon until we get it correct—which is my way and my way only."

"A *curse* on you!" raged Lady Valerie.

The ensuring silence could have been cut by a scimitar.

"Dear Valerie," said Madame Vilna, "this is the Old Avon, *not* Coven Garden." Dylan cackled. "All right, Dylan, lay your egg and then concentrate." The actor covered his mouth with his hand but his body still shook. "Now shall we take it from the top, my dears? And Dylan."

He saluted stiffly. "Yes sir!"

"When you speak your first line, "My necessaries are

embarked," there is no need to make it sound pornographic. It simply means your luggage is on board the ship and nothing else!"

Nelly Locke suddenly clutched her stomach.

"Something wrong dear?" inquired Dame Augusta, the knitting needles clicking like telegraph keys running amok.

"No . . . nothing . . . I'm all right. That woman gives me butterflies."

"Don't underestimate Madame Vilna. She's very clever. Very gifted. Very clever indeed."

Nelly's eyes travelled to the old woman. Her fingers moved nimbly though she herself was staring straight ahead to the activity on the stage. The expression on the old woman's face was one Nelly would never forget. It reminded her of an illustration in a book of fairy tales she had read as a child, a drawing of the witch in "Hansel And Gretel."

CHAPTER
three

The hotel manager unlocked the door to Edna and Sylvia's suite and gestured for them to precede him. With a theatrically elegant air, Edna swept past the young man into the room and stood in the center as though expecting a burst of applause. Behind her, Sylvia exclaimed, "Good heavens? Is this a hotel room or a plot in Kew Gardens?" The room was banked with flowers in baskets, vases, and pots.

Edna sneezed. "They have to go," she said through a sniffle, "it's hay fever season."

The young manager opened the door to their bedroom as three bellboys entered with the luggage. "In there," said Edna, her finger pointed to the bedroom as Sylvia stood at the open window glowing with appreciation of the green splendor of Hyde Park.

"I had no idea London was so beautiful!" She turned to the hotel manager. "I was terribly disappointed in Ireland when I saw it from the plane. It looks as though it's been left out in the sun too long. But this is absolutely splendid!"

Harry the chauffeur entered carrying their hat boxes, placed them on a chair, and as though by instruction, tipped the bellboys and the manager who departed in a sea of fixed smiles. Edna was on the telephone ordering tea. Sylvia sank into a couch and kicked her shoes off.

"We should let Vilna know we're here," Sylvia said to Edna, who was busy telling room service to eliminate the cucumber sandwiches as cucumbers gave her indigestion. To Harry she said, "What do we owe you for the tips?"

Mr. Gordon instructed me to take care of everything," explained Harry standing near the door with his cap under one arm.

"Oh, we couldn't let him do that!" remonstrated Sylvia.

"Why not?" asked Edna as she replaced the phone on the receiver. "All my life I've been dying to know what it's like to be kept and this is about as close as I'll ever get to it."

"I have to pick up Mr. Gordon at the BBC. That's where he tapes his daily news analysis for the States."

"Dear Joe," said Sylvia, "he's really a legend in his own time. A good reporter and a brave man. Of course, Harry, you're probably too young to remember, but his broadcasts from wartime London were absolutely spectacular. He was second only to the late Ed Murrow. He was America's youngest war correspondent. He wasn't more then twenty-three or four at the time."

"Well that was one way to beat the draft," said Edna ungraciously.

"Really, Edna! Just because he gave his book to another publisher is no reason to deprecate his accomplishments!"

"I'd better get going," said Harry. "Mr. Gordon's instructed me to be at your disposal for the length of your stay."

"Oh well, that's grand," said Edna, "we'll certainly be keeping you busy." Though it was out of her line of vision, Sylvia was positive the chauffeur's birthmark on his neck was aglow. With a smart salute, he departed. Edna lit a cigarette and sat opposite Sylvia. "We should phone the Old Avon and leave a message for Vilna."

Sylvia appeared not to hear her.

"Where are you now?" snapped Edna.

Sylvia jerked to attention. "What? Oh . . . I was thinking about the Gordons' connection to Astoroth House. It somehow seems a bit illogical."

"You want logic, read Einstein."

"Didn't you get the impression everything the chauffeur told us was rehearsed?" Edna's mouth formed a moué as she pondered the statement. "It was all so glib, so pat . . . so . . . so orderly . . . it was almost like reading those first two reports Lisa mailed me before she disappeared." Sylvia snapped her finger. "I've got news for you! He was reciting almost everything Lisa wrote!"

"Maybe she let him read them," Edna said with a Gallic shrug, "though hardly to check for grammatical errors."

"Maybe she did," agreed Sylvia, "and if she did, they must have been closer then he's let on."

"What's that got to do with the price of peas?"

"He might know a lot more than he's let on, about Lisa's disappearance that is. I'd sure like to know what Lisa told Joe Gordon that night on the phone."

"Maybe the kid was sacrificed."

"To what?"

"Satan."

"Oh stop!" Sylvia was on her feet again and pacing. "Satanic rites today are more sexual than homicidal. Most of these so-called witch cults make it up as they go along."

"There are some that take it all very seriously, Sylvia dear. I stick to my theory. Lisa must have stumbled into something dangerous to that bunch of comics at Astoroth

House. Likewise Max. A disappearance and a sudden breakdown are just too coincidental."

Sylvia was at the window again staring at Hyde Park. "You're dead right about that. There's been an awful lot of coincidences in the past couple of hours. *Nick* Hastings, *Harry* Sanders, *Astoroth* House."

"What about *Astoroth* House?"

"Astoroth is another of the Devil's aliases. Likewise Asmodeus."

"You'll never cease to amaze me. Where'd you discover those tidbits?"

Sylvia crossed back to the couch. "You didn't think I'd make this pilgrimage unprepared, did you? I've been reading up! Let me tell you, being a witch isn't like a membership in the Diner's Club."

Edna's train of thought took another direction. "Do you suppose the chauffeur bit?"

"On what?" Sylvia was reading the cards attached to the numerous floral offerings.

"Like we didn't know Vilna and that actor were at that near fatal weekend with Max?"

"It doesn't matter. We've stuck to our instructions."

(*Flush them out. I don't care how you do it. Be outrageously blunt. Make them come to you. Vilna will manage her end. It's dangerous, do you understand, girls, very dangerous. And you'll know you've struck paydirt when you get that weekend invitation to Astoroth House.*)

Edna's voice brought Sylvia back. "I think that Nick Hastings, that snotty reporter at the airport, is mixed up in this somehow."

"Of course he is. Max spotted that when he was interviewed by him. But it wasn't witchcraft that caused Lisa's disappearance. It has to be something bigger then that." She opened her purse and began thumbing her address book. "I'm going to leave a message for Vilna. The old darling, I can't wait to see her."

As the door to his office in Scotland Yard opened, Detective-Inspector Channing Roberts of Missing Persons arose from his desk, smiling heartily with his hand extended toward the first of the two visitors to enter.

"Welcome back old boy!" cried Roberts, "you're looking positively fit!"

"Thought I'd never make it," said the taller of the two priests as he warmly clasped the police officer's hand. Over his shoulder he ordered the younger, smaller priest with the hump on his back, "Shut the door, Quasi."

"Okay, okay, okay." The door slammed shut and the younger priest scuttled to a leather armchair, sat on it with his legs folded under him, drew an all-day sucker from his inside jacket pocket, tore off the wrapper and then savored with rapture the first taste of lemon-lime.

The older priest removed the black hat that had been pushed down over his ears and placed it on the desk, and then removed the thick horn-rimmed glasses and rubbed his eyes. "Ten hours of this get-up has been torture." He sat in the chair the Detective-Inspector indicated. "Quasi!"

The all-day sucker froze in mid-air.

"Say hello to Detective-Inspector Channing Roberts. He'll be working on the case with us."

"Hello, hello, hello!" said the young man, who was probably all of sixteen years of age.

"Chan, this is Quasimodo Rachmaninoff. His real name is Genghis, but due to the hump on his back, the kids back in Greenwich Village nicknamed him Quasimodo and it's stuck."

Quasimodo leaned forward. "I was once kidnapped and Max found me. I owe him a favor, so I got leave from the circus to come to London with him."

Max Van Larsen smiled. "The kid's an acrobat with Ringling Brothers. His mother should have been in touch with you by now. Have you heard from Gypsy Marie?"

"I most certainly have," said Roberts with a trace of

weariness in his voice. "She gave us quite a time helping her secure the right covered wagon and team of horses. The past three days she's been making herself known in the vicinity of Astoroth House. She's located a small tribe of fellow gypsies camped just outside the local village and reports everything's going as planned. But still no sign of Lisa, or any of the other girls who have disappeared for that matter."

"We didn't expect it to be that simple, did we?"

"No, but still, one prays for miracles."

"The ladies must be settled in at the Dorchester by now."

"Quite comfortably. I gather they did yeoman work with the press at the airport."

"I didn't catch much of it, but what little I saw looked and sounded good. I was too busy hustling us off the plane incognito. I'm pretty positive I wasn't recognized."

Roberts was at the bar behind his desk pouring Scotch. "Any aftereffects from that overdose of fly ageric?"

Max shook his head. "I hope to God never to suffer that experience again. I don't know how the acid heads survive it."

"They don't take the massive dose you were administered. It was meant to kill you, you know."

"I know. Indeed I know. Thank God Vilna was there. I still can't remember any of it. I've been told how I was spirited from Astoroth House to Joe Gordon's place. Apparently Vilna had to flatten me."

"It took me a week to convince her not to cut off her right hand," said Roberts as he brought Max his drink.

"When did Gordon bring you in?"

"While he had you at the house in a straightjacket. I arranged the male nurses and the flight to New York. I also planted the story you were hopelessly insane. How long were you out?"

"Almost a week. They were on the verge of giving up,

but some witch got into my cell with a jug of chicken soup—which she knows I loathe. *That* worked better than any of the antidotes the doctors were pumping into me. Well anyway, Chan, let's get down to it. I know it's an elaborate plot I cooked up, but I think it can work if Edna and Sylvia can hold up their end."

"It's a perfectly lovely plot *if* our suspects fall for it. And so far they seem hooked. Too early to tell for sure, of course, but Lady Valerie knows your connection with Miss Plotkin. The next step is up to her."

"I'm sure she won't let us down." Max sipped his Scotch and then smiled at Quasimodo. "Tired, kid?"

"Nope. Let's go to a strip joint."

"I'm feeding you and then sending you to your mother. You're important at her end. I want you casing Astoroth House every chance you get."

The boy winked. "You can trust Quasi."

"Don't be too cocky. There are greater dangers there than the animals in the private zoo."

Quasi made a rude gesture. "That for the animals. They eat out of my hands at the circus. They think I'm one of them."

"The person I want you to try and get close to is Lady Valerie's son, Lord Carson." He turned to Roberts. "Carson Mayhew is a blithering idiot, but don't let my opinion sway you. Actually, he's in his twenties, but since some sort of accident a few years ago, he has the mentality of a twelve-year-old." He turned to the boy. "He's no bigger then you are actually, so it's your job to make friends with him." The boy licked and nodded. "That should be the easiest way for you to get into the estate. Are you listening carefully?"

"Sure, sure." *Lick lick lick*. His tongue darted at the confection like a salamander's catching flies.

"The boy's father, Sir Vernon Mayhew, likes children, so it should be easy to weasel your way in with him."

Quasimodo nodded vigorously. "He's a doctor but they don't let him practice anymore."

"Why? He got rusty?"

"No, he got into trouble with the police a long time ago."

"Aha."

"Now he seems to do nothing but look after the zoo."

"Oho."

"The one for you to take care with is the housekeeper. She's a mean, very nasty, very evil woman." Quasimodo was now completely engrossed with Max. "Her name is Judith Sondergaard. She has one soft spot."

"Where?"

"Young Lord Carson. She dotes on him. So, through him you get to her, got it?"

"Got it."

Channing Roberts was applying a match to the bowl of his pipe. "The boy's and his mother's American accent might cause some suspicion."

"Gypsies travel the world. I think they'll get away with it."

Quasimodo rearranged himself in the chair. "Don't worry about me and mama. We know how to look after ourselves. We ain't afraid of witches. Mama can teach them a curse or two. Right, Max?"

"Right, Quasi." Max smiled and winked at Roberts who settled back.

"Will you be contacting Miss Plotkin and her companion?"

"In time. Too soon now. If they need me, they know they're to get in touch with you. Now then, any fresh leads?"

"Two fresh disappearances." Roberts told Max of two girl campers who had disappeared four days previously. Their holiday camping expedition had taken them to the village where Astoroth House was situated, Punting-On-The-Thames. They had pitched their tent about a mile down the road from the Mayhew estate, shopped for their provisions in the village, and were teen-agers.

"Like the others," commented Max sadly.

"Yes, always teen-agers. *And* always girls. That brings the total to eighteen in the past six months. Eighteen we know about, that is. Just what the link could be to Astoroth House we still can't figure out. Our spotters continue to check the black masses Lady Valerie and her aunt conduct out there, but they continue to appear harmless enough."

"That's the outdoor masses. But what goes on in that subterranean cellar?"

"There you've got me. Are you sure you didn't manage to search them that weekend?"

"I must have. The doctors tell me it'll come back to me sooner or later. I'm one of the few people you know anxious to relive a nightmare. But spare me another dose of fly ageric. Whoever thought of extracting the juice of that deadly mushroom for narcotic purposes ought to be shot."

Roberts chuckled. "Whoever did lies a long time a-mouldering in his grave. It's been known for centuries by your North American Indians. The late Aldous Huxley experimented with it in Mexico I'm told."

"That probably explains a title like 'After Many A Summer Dies The Swan,' " commented Max wrily. "How do we get the boy to his mother?"

"One of my men will deliver him there after midnight. How are your digs? Satisfactory? Sorry it has to be as far out as Islington. But then, a lot of people find it convenient to get lost in Islington. You won't be there too long anyway. You'll be receiving an invitation from the vicar at the Punting-on-the-Thames parsonage to spend the weekend with him. As soon as your friends get *their* invitation from Lady Valerie. Nice little bloke, the vicar. Writes mystery stories under a pseudonym. His name is Oscar Treble. He writes under the name of Elsie Lee Mackintosh. Read one or two of them myself, as a matter of fact." He cleared his throat. "They're absolutely filthy."

Max roared with laughter.

After their tea had been cleared away by the floor waiter, Sylvia and Edna showered and changed into housecoats. They had left a message for Madame Vilna at the Old Avon and as they were settling down with London maps and guide books, the doorbell rang. Sylvia cross the floor rapidly and admitted Joseph Gordon."

"Joe! Oh my poor Joe!" cried Sylvia as the tall man smiled, swept her into his arms, and kissed her cheek.

Edna took one look and sat erect. The years and even the recent tragedy of his daughter's disappearance had treated Joseph Gordon kindly. Over six feet in height, spare of weight, with a swarthy face and gray-streaked dark hair, he still had the commercial attractiveness of a professional male model. Edna cursed herself for not having changed into a filmy negligee.

After Edna had been introduced to Gordon, drinks were ordered and brought by the floor waiter, and then Sylvia and Gordon settled on the couch, while Edna posed provocatively in an easy chair across from them. Condolences for Lisa's disappearance and Max's breakdown were exchanged, and Sylvia amused the man briefly with a recital of her experience with the press at the airport. Although Sylvia and Edna in rotation bombarded him with questions about Lady Valerie Crawford, her aunt Dame Augusta Mayhew, Dylan Wake, and Astoroth House, they learned little more from him then they had earlier from Harry. Sylvia questioned Gordon on what she considered to be his rather strange reticence.

"What I've told you is all I know," Gordon insisted.

"Why did they close Astoroth House to the public last

year?" persisted Sylvia. "I thought it was a going concern, popular with the tourists."

"Dame Augusta couldn't stand them tramping through the grounds any longer."

"But I thought they needed that income to cover the taxes, the ground rates, the rest of the upkeep. That's a big place to keep going, isn't it?"

"Valerie and Augusta have been doing a lot of television work. And Valerie's husband has been doing well with animal breeding and selling to municipal zoos. They seem to be managing to get by."

Sylvia took his hand. "Joe darling, there's *got* to be something rotten at Astoroth. Why else Lisa's disappearance and Max being fed something that made him go berserk?"

"Are you so sure it was something Max was fed? When he arrived in London to help me find Lisa he seemed very tired and acted as though he'd been under a strain."

"That was only me. I'm *hardly* enough to send him around the bend." She didn't like the look on Edna's face at that moment but reserved comment. "The doctors think he was pumped an overdose of something called fly ageric, which is an extract of a certain species of poisonous mushroom. It could have killed him, Joe. And if it was done as a joke, then somebody has a very warped sense of humor. Max was a marked man. You didn't get any, Vilna didn't, none of the other guests did, did they?"

"No."

"Exactly. Max was the target. That means he was on to something about some hanky-panky going on up there."

Gordon sipped his drink and then spoke. "It can't be the witchcraft nonsense. Valerie got on to that for the publicity."

"I'll bet she enjoys every minute of it. Does she have a steady thirteen people in her coven?"

"To my knowledge it varies. Depends on who's available for the weekend."

Sylvia smiled winsomely. "Edna and I have been part of a coven out in East Hampton. Do you suppose we could get ourselves invited to Astoroth House as guest witches?"

"I'm sure Valerie would be delighted to have you. She's certainly heard a great deal about you from Madame Vilna and myself . . . "

" . . . And Max," added Sylvia flatly.

"Oh, there was nothing to that," hastened Gordon. "After all, there's Sir Vernon, Valerie's husband."

"I hear he's just around for show."

"Oh no. They're still quite fond of each other."

"There's fond and there's *fond*. Sir Vernon's a de-frocked doctor. Maybe he was jealous of Max and slipped him the mickey."

"I don't see how. It happened at lunch. Vernon was at the head of the table, Valerie at the foot. Max sat on Valerie's right hand and Vilna sat on her left hand."

"How did she eat?" queried Edna sharply, "through a tube?"

"Please, Edna." Edna was delighted they hadn't recognized the line as stolen from Groucho Marx. "Where was Max sitting?"

"I told you. At Valerie's right. And Dylan Wake—he's an actor . . . "

"We've been through that."

"Oh yes . . . of course . . . he sat on Max's other side. Max had just finished his soup when he started convulsing."

"Oh, my poor Max. My poor heavenly baby. What kind of soup?"

"Well, come to think of it, it was cream of mushroom."

"Aha!" Sylvia leapt to her feet and Gordon almost spilled his drink. Sylvia began pacing the room with her hands on her hips, Mother Courage on the loose again. "Cream of *mushroom* soup!" She halted in the center of the room and faced Gordeon. "What went on that weekend?"

"What do you mean?"

"Anything out of the ordinary occur?"

"No. There was the usual black mass at midnight on Saturday. Max seemed rather amused by it. Otherwise, it was like any ordinary weekend at Astoroth House."

"Wasn't Max asking questions about the weekend that Lisa disappeared?"

"Subtly, yes."

Edna was studying the man carefully. There's something wrong, she thought to herself. Something very wrong. His one and only beloved daughter is missing, and yet he behaves like he's about to embark on a fishing trip. I'm going to get to the bottom of him, and for a man in his early fifties, he has a very cute bottom. She wriggled forward in her seat.

"Do you know you have very beautiful hands?"

Gordon blushed.

"But you do. Doesn't he, Sylvia darling?" Sylvia wasn't sure what Edna was up to, but instinct from past experience told her to follow Edna's lead.

Sylvia folder her arms. "They should be cast in bronze."

Edna restrained from wincing and favored Gordon with her most provocative, seductive, engaging smile. "I don't know *why* I should be paying you compliments when you gave your book of wartime reminiscences to a rival publishing house. But I'm such an aesthete, such a lover of beauty, and I play bridge a great deal and so I can't help noticing hands and yours are so beautifully tapered and sensitive." Gordon refrained from telling her at the moment that his fingers were ice cold.

"Could I have another drink?" The words stumbled from his mouth like a parade of spastics.

"Edna, stop embarrassing Joe!" cried Sylvia as she crossed to Gordon, took his glass, and refilled it with vodka and tonic.

"Oh, I'm not at *all*! Am I, Joe?"

"Hell no." He tugged at his collar which seemed to have tightened around his neck in the past thirty seconds.

The phone rang.

Edna, who was nearest to it, arose langurously and with a coquettish look at Gordon, swivel-hipped to the desk and then spoke seductively into the mouthpiece. "Hell-oh-oh-oh?"

From the other end she heard a booming, "So, who are you making a play for now, you *nofka?*"

"Vilna darling!" shreiked Edna. "Sylvia, it's Vilna! Vilna come over this second! This very minute!"

In Paddy, the stagdoorkeeper's office at the Old Avon, Vilna glared at the telephone she was holding. "I am in the middle of a rehearsal, you stupid editor. We are merely having a tea break—a most unnecessary custom peculiar to this country—but when in Rome etceter*ah*, and so I have taken the opportunity to reciprocate your message. How's Max?" She listened attentively and nodded with pleasure, out of the corner of her eye spotting Dylan Wake and Nelly Locke deep in conversaton in the Green Room across the passage from Paddy's office. "Give me Sylvia. I *hunger* for the sound of her voice."

As she waited for Sylvia to take over from Edna, she subtly eyed the two youngsters in the other room. There is something wrong there, she thought. Something very, very wrong there. This is quite obvious from the tears streaming down Nelly's cheeks.

CHAPTER
four

"Vilna, Vilna, Vilna *darling*!" crowed Sylvia into the phone, while Joe Gordon wondered whether an egg might drop.

"Hearken, she *speaks*!" yodeled Madame Vilna from her end. "That voice! That anodyne for my ailing soul! To hear your voice is like Passover out of season!"

The door to the Green Room slammed shut.

The weird smile Dylan Wake sported wasn't so much set as newly repaired. The muscles around his mouth twitched and at least two of the alcoholic veins seemed about to pop.

"You're joking, of course," he said to Nelly as she attempted to staunch the flow of tears with the palms of her hands.

"I'm not. You *know* I'm not. You've got to do something."

He turned his back on her and crossed to a table where earlier he had left a half-finished bottle of beer, picking it up, and clenching it tightly in his right fist as though it was a potential lethal weapon. "You've tried to pull this on me before. I haven't forgotten that."

"I don't want the damned baby any more then you do!"

Dylan took a swig of beer, ran it around his mouth for a few seconds, as though undecided between swallowing or inundating the girl. He swallowed, suppressed a belch, and then faced her. Very softly he told her, "You're a bloody idiot. It'll take a hundred quid at least and where the hell do I get that?"

"You know where." Her eyes blazed a heady mixture of knowledge and defiance. "*She'll* give you the money."

Dylan began walking around the room, swirling the remaining beer in the bottle until a thin layer of foam appeared, studying the portraits of theatrical immortals that decorated the walls of the Green Room. He paused under a painting of Edmund Kean silently identifying, as he frequently did with the late tortured genius. Over his shoulder he said in a half whisper, "My account's overdrawn."

"That's *your* problem."

He spun around with a ferocity that made her recoil. "Bloody bitch!" he shouted, "Bloody whore!"

Nelly held her ground with the bravery and arrogance peculiar only to ambitious young actresses. "I've heard the same said of you. You work this out. I don't care how you do it, as long as you *do*. And *quick*!" Her tiny fists were clenched and beating the air and Dylan was smart enough to recognize a Mexican standoff when he saw one.

There was a brisk rap at the door before flung open and Madame Vilna entered grinning from ear to ear. "Forgive the intrusion, my slaves, but you, Dylan, are whom I am seeking!" She stopped short and clenched her hands in a mocking gesture. "Aha! I feel the air is charged with electricity! I feel a tension I have not felt since that night I stepped upon the stage in *Ehr Hutt Nisht Kein Saychel*, which is perhaps more familiar to you as *The Simpleton Of The Unexpected Isles*. If the moment is not opportune, forgive this old goddess of all she surveys . . . "

Nelly fled the room and Vilna halted in mid-sentence. Her right foot shot out nimbly, connecting with the door which closed with a groan as Vilna's head wagged from side to side in reproof. *"Now* what?"

"Me old darlin', you couldn't possibly give me a hundred pounds?"

"From my body, yes, from my purse, no. How many months pregnant is she?"

"Probably two. It's nothing new to her."

Vilna suggested airily, "Perhaps at last you should marry her and settle down."

"To what?"

"You don't love her?"

"All that I love stands before you."

"Somehow, I feel if you ever had the courage to investigate yourself, you would find that you do love her. But then, one does not find courage at a frozen food counter. Tell me, my dormant potential, are you perhaps available for this evening to myself and two adorable friends recently arrived from abroad?

"The Plotkin lady?" he inquired with a mixture of curiosity and eagerness.

"The sylvan Sylvia herself! She is gaily ensconced at the Dorchester Hotel with her friend and misadviser Edna St. Thomas Shelley, and I thought perhaps you might care to join a small party, as the guest of course of our friend Joseph Gordon. I find myself with such a paucity of amusing young men in my immediate and restricted circle, and I know you could always use a good meal. Dare we hope to include you?"

His face was aglow like Christmas. "Why not? Why not indeed me old darlin'! Is she still spoken for by me old mate Van Larsen?"

"A whisper lingers on, yes."

His voice sobered. "How is Max?"

"He shall survive." Vilna was staring at her right hand. "To think, "she waved the hand in front of her face with

51

revulsion, "to think this flesh struck the last surviving male for whom I harbor a modicum of respect! But, of course, you were present at that infamous moment and only too well recognized the emergency." She shook her head sadly as she lowered the hand. "I had not struck another human being since that climactic moment in the third act of *Eine Naya Maidel*, which is perhaps more familiar to you as *Born Yesterday*. Enough! Enough!" Her face brightened and for a moment Dylan wished (as he had frequently wished from the moment he had first encountered Madame Vilna two months earlier) that she was thirty years younger.

"Enough, enough, enough!" she repeated with both hands flailing as though cutting off a dentist and his drill, "we will meet this evening at seven o'clock *sharp* at the Plotkin Suite at the Dorchester. You will attempt of course for the first thirty minutes to comport yourself like a civilized gentleman, and *not* like an actor."

"I love you," he said with a rare sincerity.

Vilna patted his cheek gently. "I understand, you sadly impetuous, romantic fool, but Vilna belongs to the *world*!" She swept to the door, pulled it open, and disappeared down the gangway to the stage.

Dylan downed the remainder of the beer, chucked the bottle into a wastepaper basket, plunged his hands into both pockets, and whistling merrily, followed in the wake of Madame Vilna.

Fifty miles from London on a lonely tree-lined road that led to the front gates of Astoroth House, two chestnut-colored horses pulling a covered wagon reacted briskly to the smart snap of a whip that cracked over their flanks and lurched forward accelerating to a brisk trot.

On the wagon seat, Gypsty Marie Rachmaninoff held tight to the reins with her left hand as she wielded the whip with the right. "Go, you basterds, go!" she shouted, "make like *Ben Hur*!"

Clip-Clop Clip-Clop Clip-Clop. To Gypsy Marie's ears, the sound of the hoofs connecting with the dirt road was Ravel's "Bolero." She was a handsome woman in her early forties, her lightly tanned skin accenting her lovely hazel eyes, aquiline nose, and magenta lips. Her hair was enswathed by a bright red bandanna and from her ears dangled brass crescents. She wore a freshly laundered orange blouse and a red velvet vest. Her ample skirt, which billowed when she walked, was decorated with the twelve signs of the zodiac, all neatly embroidered by her own professional hand.

Ahead of her, beyond a six-foot high brick wall, loomed the vast architectural expanse of Astoroth House. It was three stories high and seemed a quarter of a mile in width, nestling in the heart of sixty acres of land. A vast maze of trees and bushes separated the building from the private zoo, spread out over two acres of land. Even now, Gypsy Marie could hear the cacophanous symphony of animal cries and roars. She squared her shoulders and sent the whip whistling again.

The gates to the cobbled road leading to the front of Astoroth House were ajar and Gypsy Marie directed her one-woman caravan accordingly. She could see a figure standing at a window adjacent to the huge oak doors that provided the front access to the house. Marie's telescopic vision discerned a tall woman dressed completely in black, hands folded sternly in front of her, black hair tightly braided in a crown, black shawl over the shoulders, and dangling from her waist, a black chain shackling dozens of assorted keys.

The horses came to a halt, Marie braked the wagon, and then wrapped the reins around a short pole. Slowly, she climbed down the wagon as one of the two oak doors slowly swung ajar. In the doorway appeared the woman in black. Gypsy Marie was unprepared for such striking, exotic beauty. She knew at once from the description given her that this would be the housekeeper, Judith

Sondergaard. The woman stood like the dog Cerberus guarding the portals of the infernal regions. When she spoke, Gypsy Marie realized sadly Judith Sondergaard's beauty was restricted to her exterior. Her voice was about as melodious as a tin can filled with broken glass.

"You're trespassing!"

Gypsy Marie folded her arms and took two steps forward. "Have you anything for the gypsy?"

"We do not permit beggars here."

Gypsy Marie was a past master at the art of storming female battlements. The smile she mustered oozed chocolate sauce. "I do not come to beg, I come to barter."

Judith Sondergaard made a move to go back into the house.

"Wait!"

Judith's hand froze to the door.

"I see a cloud above your head."

Judith's grip tightened on the door.

"It is a black cloud." Gypsy Marie's right foot was on the first stone step leading up to the house. "And not an ordinary cloud either." Her voice rumbled like thunder. "It's oblong. It is shaped like a coffin."

Gypsy Marie heard the sound of a river boat chugging up the Amazon and decided the woman was laughing.

"Do not mock Gypsy Marie Rachmaninoff," she admonished, adding the sign of the cross for good measure, "I have foreseen with amazing and uncontested accuracy the future of many great celebrities! In Greenwich Village I am adored and respected by a select circle of queens. I have a rare autographed photograph of Norman Mailer and William Buckley—*together*. Divine providence directed me across the Atlantic Ocean to this country, in addition to the advice of a friendly agent with William Morris." She stroked her chin and then inquired with Bohemian sincerity, "Have you ever been in the movies?"

"You must be mad!"

"But you are intrigued, no?" Gypsy Marie could always sense when her invisible net was tightening around a sucker.

Judith Sondergaard's stern demeanor began to relax and even her voice softened to a clatter of cow bells. "What are you selling, not that we need anything?"

"Not *we*," corrected Gypsy Marie as her finger stabbed the air, "*you*. You are troubled. You need advice. Dark deeds have been perpetrated in the bowels of this vast mansion. I *know*. I can sense it. This is a house," she added darkly, "that harbors mockery. Yes, yes . . ." she had made it to the fourth stone step with six more to go, "and I sense that you feel constricted by it! You are still a young and very passionate woman, but there is a girdle not of your design constricting and stifling your passion. I can see the bulges! Ooops! That dark cloud has dropped an inch."

"You have an intriguing line of patter."

"You ain't heard nothing yet, Miss Sondergaard." Were she comfortably positioned, she might have kicked herself. Sondergaard came to her rescue.

"Everyone in the village knows me. I'm sure you prepared yourself before coming here."

Joe Namath would have envied Gypsy Marie's agile sidestep. "I want to tell your fortune. The crystal ball, the Tarot cards, the palm of your hand. I have a feeling you need all the help I can give you. Invite me in. You will have no regrets." Marie's voice was hypnotic. "Invite me in."

Behind the house on a path in the maze that separated Astoroth House from the zoo, stunted Lord Carson Mayhew was fiercely propelling his scooter with one foot, both hands tightly clutching the handlebars, head projecting forward like the figurehead on an ancient

Roman barque. Although in his mid-twenties, his diminutive size gave him the appearance of a child of twelve. His long flaxen hair hanging to his shoulders gave him a look of a cavalier of yore. The unnatural prettiness of his face was marred by a jagged scar that ran from his left eye to the top of his left ear.

"Daddy, daddy, daddy, daddy!" his voice pierced like a bosun's whistle, "come quick, daddy, come quick!"

Sir Vernon Mayhew, who was forcing a side of corroded beef through the bars of a lion cage with a long pole, straightened up and mopped his brow with the sleeve of his shirt. He was a man in his early fifties with a craggy, masculine attractiveness and thin but muscular body.

"Stop that yelling, Carson!" he yelled, "you know your voice puts the animals off their feed!"

"But daddy! Daddy! There's a unicorn chasing me!"

Sir Vernon, who was facing a glaring sunlight, squinted past his son. "Oh now really, Carson, you do go on a bit, lad."

"It's a unicorn! A unicorn!" He whizzed past his father, lost his balance and tumbled head first into a pile of hay.

"Oh my gawd!" shouted Sir Vernon as a rhinoceros came lumbering into view, "Rosie's loose again! Tom! Hank! Mervyn!" he shouted to the assistant zoo-keepers scattered about the compound, "Get that stupid bitch back where she belongs!" The men came running from three directions as Sir Vernon raced to the pile of hay.

"You all right, sonny?" he inquired with affection as he pulled his son out of the hay by the waist.

"Carson frightened, Da . . . Carson *frightened*!"

The older man held his son tightly. "It's all right, son. It's all right. Rosie's harmless. she wouldn't hurt you."

"Carson frightened," he kept repeating, "Carson frightened." His face was hidden against his father's chest. Sir Vernon stroked the flaxen hair along the side of his head, and then his fingers felt the scar.

"Daddy won't ever let any harm come to you again, not ever again."

"Promise?"

"I promise."

Carson moved his head back and stared into his father's face with a giggle.

"I don't want to play with Rosie. I want to play with girls. When can I have another girl to play with?"

Sir Vernon held the boy's face in his hands. "Soon."

"*How* soon?"

"Soon. I promise you."

"Carson loves his daddy," piped the tiny voice.

"Daddy loves his Carson."

Then Carson's hands flew to his scar as his face contorted with unbearable agony. "Oh it hurt! It hurt! Daddy make the hurt stop. It hurt! It hurt!"

Sir Vernon pressed the boy even tighter to his body. *Oh, that bastard. I'll get that bastard for this. I'll kill him one day for doing this to you. And when the time comes, they won't stop me. The next time . . . they won't stop me.*

The kitchen at Astoroth House was large enough to accomodate a hockey game. At a table, Judith Sondegaard and Gypsy Marie Rachmaninoff sat across from each other. Between them was a crystal ball and Gypsy Marie's Tarot cards carefully dealt and laid out. Miss Sondergaard's hands were flat on the table palms upward. Gypsy Marie in special cases brought all her guns to bear. Her eyes darted from ball to cards to upturned palms.

"As I suspected," said Gypsy Marie in a voice barely audible, "you are a network of complexities." She looked up and locked eyes with the housekeeper. "For many months you have suffered with a severe inner struggle. Your origins are Scandinavian, are they not?"

Judith Sondergaard nodded.

"Yes, there is no denying that. There is an arrow in the crystal ball pointing north." She peered closer into the crystal. "This is hardly pertinent, but it's going to rain."

"Oh, this is ridiculous!"

"Unclench you fists!" Slowly, the fists unclenched. "That's better. You were once the headmistress of a school."

"I was not!"

"Do not lie! Mendacity is no match for my supernatural powers! You have been involved in some way with young girls!" Gypsy Marie tapped the crystal ball with an amazingly well-manicured fingernail. "Were you ever a Rockette?"

Judith Sondergaard snorted.

Gypsy Marie persisted. "I see you with teen-age girls." She cocked her head. "Perhaps you took young girls on guided tours or something similar?"

"Why . . . why yes, as a matter of fact. But that was years ago."

Gypsy Marie clapped her hands triumphantly. "Score one for me." She peered back into the crystal ball. "You *were* once an actress."

"Yes," admitted Miss Sondergaard almost shyly, "but I was inadequate."

"But it brought you in contact with someone who resides in this house."

"Everybody knows Astoroth House belongs to Dame Augusta Mayhew!"

"It is not she who brought you here. It was another."

"Yes. Lady Valerie Crawford. I was on the road with her years ago in an unsuccessful tour of a German play, *Maedchen In Uniform*."

"Ah! Didn't *that* involve teen-age girls?" Gypsy Marie silently thanked God for the Art Theatre in New York's Greenwich Village where she had recently seen a revival of the film version of the play starring Dorothea Weick.

"Why yes . . . of course . . . you're quite clever."

"I work very hard." Gypsy Marie leaned forward conspiratorially. "So far, I have merely skimmed the surface of my powers. When I come to the rare but occasional bind," she looked over her shoulders to make sure they were still alone, "I bring into play a bit of . . . *sorcery*." Gypsy Marie smiled. "In certain quarters back in New York, I am known as the Witch of West Houston Street. Have you heard of me?"

"I'm afraid I haven't."

Gypsy Marie shrugged. "You might have if I could afford a press agent. *Ah!*"

"What is it?" Judith Sondergaard asked hungrily.

Hooked, thought Gypsy Marie with lavish pleasure, *absolutely hooked*.

"I see unrequited love." She thought she detected a slight trembling in the other woman's hands.

Said Judith Sondergaard in a strained voice, "Unrequited love's a bore."

"You can sing that in high C if you like, but a fact is a fact."

The housekeeper abruptly pushed her chair from the table and towered over Gypsy Marie. "I have had enough." Each word was a knife thrust.

Gypsy Marie nodded without looking up as she gathered the cards together into a neat pile. "Yes. Even though we have barely scraped the surface of your complexities. The first session is always the most painful."

"How much do I owe you?"

"You owe me nothing."

"You're a very poor business woman."

Gypsy Marie whipped a black knitted bag from a large pocket in her skirt and as she placed the crystal ball in it said, looking straight into Judith Sondergaard's eyes, "For a first session, this has been much too unsatisfactory. Gypsy Marie Rachmaninoff is a *perfectionist.*" The last word emerged from her mouth like escaping steam. "I will come again."

"I don't think so."

"You have no choice, my dear."

"I beg your pardon!"

"You don't, you know. I shall come again. You will send for me." She was standing lightly juggling the wrapped crystal ball in her right hand. "It will be an irresistible compulsion. Mark my words, as I use them sparingly—contrary to a general opinion I have learned to ignore. I shall be camped with the gypsies about a mile down the road. You've seen them?"

"Yes. They're a nuisance."

"Only because they are Hungarian gypsies. The others are out of season. I am waiting there to be joined by my child. My daughter Salmonella.

"Strange name for a girl."

"She's a very strange daughter. Tragically, she was born hunchbacked. But she has an extremely loving nature that permeates and goes right through you. She is a most amazing teen-ager. She *too* has the power. She was born with a caul. I go now. Until next we meet. *Au revoir . . .* Judith Sondergaard . . . *Au revoir.*"

Gypsy Marie left through the front of the house as Sir Vernon entered the kitchen from the rear door, catching a glimpse of the fortuneteller from behind as she departed.

"Who was that?" he asked the housekeeper.

"A gypsy woman. Quite an amusing character." She smiled provocatively. "Would you like something to eat?"

"Yes," he said softly as his eyes devoured her, "yes, I would." He strode across the room, pulled her into his arms and kissed her passionately.

CHAPTER
five

After Sylvia concluded her chat with Madame Vilna and hung up the phone, she turned to Edna and Joseph Gordon with a smile of elation. "It's all arranged for tonight. We're to meet here at seven for cocktails and then we go on the town! London, look out! Is that all right with you, Joe? I mean we're not taking you away from anything important, are we?"

"What could be more important then you, Sylvia?" asked Gordon with flattering gallantry.

"Vilna invited that actor chap, Dylan Wake, to join us. Is that all right, Joe?"

Sylvia thought she heard a creaking hinge as Gordon's jaw dropped.

"Is something wrong?"

"Why, no! No! He's a charming fellow, a bit much at times, but a charming fellow."

Edna folded her hands across her ample chest and said gravely, "You're a very brave man, Joseph Gordon."

"Nonsense! I'm looking forward to tonight."

"That's not what I'm referring to. That you could enter freely into our project rollicking and frolicking with the feigned eagerness of a terminal case at a bar mitzvah, when inside you I can hear the drip, drip, drip, of your private tears." Sylvia's eyes searched wildly for something like a butterfly net and settled instead for the bottle of Scotch. "You are wonderful, bearing up so magnificently under the strain of your tragedy. But then, almost all your life you've walked hand in hand with tragedy. They say the eyes are the window of the soul." Edna leaned forward for a closer scrutiny of his eyes and balanced herself with one hand firmly clutching his right knee.

"Urmph."

"In your eyes, Joe, I see equal dollops of pain and suffering. Don't you want to *talk* about Lisa? Sylvia and I are women," the women briefly exchanging reassuring glances, "and though we have never been mothers— "she paused pregnantly, "to my knowledge—we understand the loss of a daughter."

"Freshen up your drink, Joe?" inquired Sylvia graciously.

"No, I'm fine, just fine." The portion of his knee where Edna's hand rested felt like an oast at full blaze. To Edna he said, "It isn't easy to talk about Lisa. The initial shock is past and, frankly, every time I think about her I feel helplessly impotent."

"I can't imagine you impotent," murmured Edna, "ever." She leaned back and Gordon straightened his leg. "I think Max was very hot on her trail when they slipped him that mickey. Perhaps you don't know what Max is like when he's following a trail. He's like a stalking panther. Stealthy, stalwart, unflagging . . . " She heard Sylvia sniffling. "Don't get maudlin, Sylvia. I'm talking about Max, not the present administration." Edna's eyes found Gordon again. "Didn't Lisa have a boy friend?"

Gordon was staring into his half-empty glass.

"From Sylvia's description when Lisa visited New York last Christmas, I drew a portrait of a very pretty young lady."

"Lisa was a very popular girl."

Was, thought Sylvia. Past tense? Has he given up hope? Has he written her off? Does a father ever write off a daughter except on his income tax or when he's paid for the wedding?

"Oh not *was*, Joe, not *was*," implored Sylvia with the fervor of a fundraiser for the United Jewish Appeal, "you can't have given up hope."

"I'll never give up hope," countered Gordon staunchly, "never. But . . . well . . . " he placed his glass on an end table, "I've been around a long time and I guess I've almost seen it all. You have to be realistic, prepare for the inevitable. I have to face the fact I may never see her again. It's over a month since her disappearance."

"Did she have much money with her?" pressed Edna.

"I haven't the vaguest idea. How much cash do you take with you to a weekend at a private home?"

"Depends on your host," advised Edna as she patted her hair. "What about her bank account? Any large withdrawals?"

"No. She didn't have all that much to withdraw. She's been living mostly on the allowance I give her."

"You don't live together?" That was Sylvia.

"Oh, not for months. When she got back from America, she took this flat with another girl in Chelsea, off King's Road."

"What about her flatmate? Wasn't she any help?"

"Nelly?" Joe smiled ruefully. "Nelly's got problems of her own." He stared at Sylvia. "Ask Madame Vilna about Nelly Locke. She's an actress. Lady Valerie's understudy."

"Well, *what* a coincidence!" Sylvia could feel the blood rushing to her face.

"Nelly's a good kid," Gordon continued, "talented girl. She and Lisa had— " Sylvia clucked her tongue, "*have* a lot in common. I suppose they shared the same boyfriends."

"Anybody you've met?" Edna was fingering a strand of beads around her neck, unaware that Gordon was privately wishing they were the wrong end of a noose.

"Well, yes," said Gordon rubbing his hands along the sides of his thighs, "Dylan Wake."

"Well, well, well." Edna sounded like a xylophone badly in need of tuning. "Now I'm *really* looking forward to meeting that young man. And he was a guest at Max's near-fatal weekend. From the expression on your face, Joe, I get the feeling you're not too partial to young Wake."

"He's not exactly my cup of tea."

"Oh dear," said Sylvia, "and now you're forced to put up with him this evening. Oh dear, oh dear, how terrible."

"Not at all," said Gordon jauntily, "it doesn't bother me a bit. And talking about this evening," he glanced at his wristwatch, "I'd better get home and change."

The phone rang and Sylvia answered as Edna took Gordon's arm and walked him to the door, gently patting his hand for the distance. "You know," she said coyly, "you've lived up to almost all my preconceived ideas about you."

"Ha, ha, ha." The laughter seemed to be coming from an echo chamber.

"How long ago was it your wife passed away?"

"She didn't pass away, she passed out. She died an alcoholic. Lisa was still an infant at the time."

"Your back must be scarred from the crosses you bear." She pulled his head down and gently rewarded his cheek with the gift of her blazing lips. "Edna's salve," she whispered, "just a stingy little sample."

"See you later, Joe!" shouted Sylvia from the desk as she replaced the telephone. She wondered what made him stagger past the door Edna was holding open. He waved a hand feebly and disappeared. Edna closed the door and jet-propelled her way to the center of the room.

"I can't stand enigmas," she fumed. "That's an enigma that Joseph Gordon."

"Oh for crying out loud, Edna, he's always been that way. He's always been shy and introverted and passive. Why else would he be Max's friend?" She thought for a moment. "Quite a contradiction though, isn't it. The brave foreign correspondent, the terror of foreign affairs." Her train of thought jumped the track. "I'm looking forward to this Dylan Wake."

"Yeah," mused Edna, "I can't wait to see this symbol of fatal fascination. Lady Valerie, Nelly whatever, Lisa even our own beloved Vilna, all seemingly kneeling in obeisance in his direction. For crying out loud, what's he supposed to be, Mecca?"

Sylvia paused, then said, "That was Detective-Inspector Roberts on the phone."

"Oh?" responded Edna eagerly, "and when do we meet *him*?"

"In about ten minutes. He's on his way over."

"I must change into a negligee!"

"What for? He's a policeman, not a talent scout."

The stage at the Old Avon was deserted except for Sir Leonard Greystoke downstage center staring at the ceiling, his right hand tightly gripping a burning candle.

" *'To be . . . or not to be . . . that is the question . . .'*"

"Sir Leonard, darling!" interrupted Madame Vilna from the rear of the stalls, "what's with the candle? You're lost?"

Greystoke squinted through his glowering countenance but could not see his director. "It is for an effect!" He shouted in a voice that belied the frailty of his aged body.

"It has been done by a previous Sir!" bellowed Vilna. "Olivier in his film played with a candle. *You* watched

Olivier? *I* watched the candle!" She was coming down the aisle placing each foot before her like a pile-driver. "You will look to Vilna for your effects! I do not wish my actors to think for *themselves*. Blow out that rotten taper or are you perhaps expecting a chorus of *Happy birthday*?"

In a rare outburst, Sir Leonard hurled the candle to the floor and began hopping up and down on it. "I hate her! I hate her! I hate her!" he shrieked.

"Enough!" shouted Vilna, "I will have no dancing during my rehearsal! Enough I say! I hate that rotten soliloquy anyway! It stops the plot cold! I shall excise it instantly!"

"*What*? gasped Sir Leonard. He staggered forward. "Are you mad?"

"Mad? I? Vilna?" She was now at the bottom of the aisle looking up into the actor's apoplectic face. "Vilna has not been mad since her sterling triumph many decades ago in *Shluff, Shluff, Alte Veiber*, which is perhaps more familiar to you as *Ladies In Retirement*. Sir Leonard? Sir Leonard darling, why are you choking and blue in the face? *Guttenyoo!* He's having an attack!"

The company came rushing onstage from all directions as Vilna took the makeshift stairs by twos. Lady Valerie and Dylan Wake were the first to reach the old man.

"Drink this, old boy," Vilna heard someone say as a paper cup was held to Greystoke's lips. The old man managed a mouthful, swallowed, and then struggled to breathe.

"A doctor!" shouted Vilna, "procure a doctor *immediatement*!" She shoved the others aside, knelt beside the old man, and cradled him in her arms, one hand deftly loosening his tie and collar. "Gently, old darling," she said in a soothing voice that disguised her inner panic, "gently, sweetheart, gently. Vilna was only joking. Vilna is always making jokes. Why she even once unexpectedly tore the house down as Pesha in *Ich Vill Dehargenen Meine Techter*, which is perhaps more familiar to you as *The House Of Bernarda Alba*."

Sir Leonard Greystoke twitched and expired.

"Sir Leonard?" pleaded Vilna as her eyes brimmed with tears. "Sir Leonard? Sir?" She bellowed, "*Lenny!*"

Dylan Wake relieved Vilna of her burden. Very gently, he straightened the body on the floor, removed his leather jacket, and covered the face. He clasped his hands, raised his head, and oblivious to the surrounding chaos recited, "*Now cracks a noble heart. Good night, sweet prince, . . . and flights of angels sing thee to thy rest!*"

He heard a snort, turned and glared at Dame Augusta Mayhew.

"What have I done?" wailed Madame Vilna, "what have I done?"

Dylan Wake knelt beside her, picking up the paper cup that had been held to Greystoke's lips, and crushing it in his hands as he spoke. "Don't fret, me old darlin'. He died with his boots on, in harness. He was a very old man. He's had a heart condition for years."

"My dear," interposed Dame Augusta, "these rehearsals have been a struggle for him. He was much too valiant, too brave, and too miserably egotistical to admit he'd never make it to opening night. And I assure you, those rejuvenation treatments in Switzerland sapped more out of him then they instilled. In other words, dear Madame Vilna, he's had it."

But Madame Vilna was inconsolable. "How will I live with myself? How? *How?*" Dylan and Lady Valerie were helping her to her feet.

"Get her a drink!" someone suggested.

"Seltzer," whispered Madame Vilna.

"Bring a chair, you bloody fools!" Dylan ordered over his shoulder. A chair was brought and Vilna was eased on to it. She clung tightly to Dylan's hand.

"Well, buddy boy, this is it."

"What?"

"Your new opportunity." Lady Valerie went white. "*You*, my Dylan, shall play Hamlet."

Nelly Locke stared at the tiny pool of water near the dead man's head, the last dregs from the paper cup.

"Jesus," whispered Dylan, "Sweet Jesus . . . *me* . . . Hamlet . . . "

"*You!*" Vilna had regained her strength and leapt to her feet, just as in the distance was heard the combined wailing of police and ambulance sirens. "Clear the stage!" She pointed to the corpse. "Remove him! The show must go on!" She bent over and spoke to the body. "As an old trooper you will understand, Sir Leonard, my darling. Farewell." She straightened and clapped her hands together. "Attention! Attention please! *Ah-tahn-see-own!* My children! The theatre is symbolized by its two masks—laughter and tragedy! Today we have had occasion to chuckle and to weep! Now we *work!*"

Several constables came rushing onstage followed by two ambulance attendants bearing a stretcher. Vilna beamed at the ambulance attendants. "You darling creatures. Please clear the stage."

Nelly Locke sidled up to Dylan Wake and whispered viciously, "*You bastard.*"

To the north in a cramped bed-sitting room in Islington, a rebellious Quasimodo Rachmaninoff stood cornered between the bed and a dresser, brandishing an umbrella with menace.

"I won't! I won't! I won't!" he shouted. "I won't wear it, damn it!"

Between two fingers of each hand, Max Van Larsen held up the dress like a sacred standard. "Are you going to let the team down, Quasi?"

"I ain't getting into drag and that's *that*!"

"It's a disguise, damn it!" growled Max ferociously.

"Then *you* wear it."

"It's too small for me. Come on Quasi, Roberts' boys are picking you up soon. Damn it you're letting your mother down! Think of *that*! She's set the stage for a daughter and you're it!"

"I don't like the color."

"Will you please lower that umbrella and come over here and talk to me, man to man. *Please*."

Slowly, the umbrella came to half-mast and then the hunchbacked boy pouted his way to Max.

"Come on, feller, you've always known this was part of the job. Look, it's play acting see? Little Lord Carson likes little girls and that's how you'll make friends with him, get it?"

"Yeah? And what happens when he tries to put his hand under my skirt?"

"He'll get an unexpected surprise. Besides, little virgins learn to keep their legs together."

"Not in the circus," amended Quasimodo with a leer.

"Put it on!" commanded Max in a voice unfamiliar to the boy. Slowly, he dropped the umbrella, raised his hands, and Max slipped the dress over his head. He stood back and surveyed the finished product professionally. "Very good. Not bad at all. In fact you're real cute."

Quasimodo's reply is unprintable.

Max crossed to an open suitcase and removed a wig. He crossed to the groaning boy, placed it on his head, and adjusted it until he was satisfied.

"Great!" exclaimed Max. He led the boy by the hand to a floor-length mirror.

"Oy!" cried Quasimodo at his reflection. "Mary Pickford!"

A fringe of blond bangs reached to his eyebrows, and a cluster of yellow curls hung to his chin line like limp sausages.

"Okay, Max, tell me this," said the boy gruffly.

"What?"

"Do I take the pill?"

Detective-Inspector Channing had found a rapt and attentive audience in Sylvia and Edna. In a seemingly brief space of fifteen minutes, he had fleshed out the plot Max had briefly sketched for them the previous evening in New York. Sylvia had clucked her tongue in shock and sympathy at the number of missing teen-age girls reported over the past six months.

"But that many girls to disappear into thin air . . . and without a *trace*!"

"Well, not exactly without a trace," corrected Roberts, as he tapped his pipe bowl in an ash tray and refilled it with a sweet-smelling mixture of tobacco. "Interpol is working closely with us. You see, there's apparently a number of similar situations cropping up on the Continent. Naturally, they assume there's a link to our problems here."

Edna was adoring his Oxford (she assumed) accent, his Savile Row suit (it certainly looked it), his well-manicured nails (a sartorial cop, too *much*) and his all-around calm, charming savoir-faire. She'd never cruised anything like this back at Whyte's in New York. She wondered, among other things, if there was a book in him.

"Of course, we mustn't jump to any hasty conclusions," Robert was saying as he torched the tobacco, "but it does have the appearance of organized crime."

"You mean like the *Mafia?*" said Sylvia darkly.

"What Mafia?" snapped Edna. "Haven't you seen the papers? An army of Italian citizens in America marched on the F.B.I. claiming there ain't no Mafia." She admired the fingernails of her right hand against her negligee. "And here I'm stuck with a book by a historian who names Marco Polo and Christopher Columbus."

"You're getting warm," said Roberts. "If Interpol's theory is correct, these girls are being shipped to Africa and the Far East as prostitutes."

"Oh, how *awful*!" cried Sylvia.

"Especially if you don't dig Chinamen," added Edna with practicality.

"For goodness' *sake*!" Sylvia sounded as though she had just run into a long-lost relative during ladies' night at a Turkish bath. "But white slavery is so old *hat*! I mean for Doctor Fu Man Chu it's just dandy, but in *this* day and age?"

"My dear Miss Plotkin," said Robert condescendingly, "you are naive."

"Listen Detective-Inspector," said Sylvia wearily, "I didn't know I was a girl until some smart-ass kid on my block looked up my dress and asked me where I got the scar."

Edna leaned forward. "But how do they—whoever they are and so to speak—*recruit* these girls, short of kid-napping?"

"Most of these girls have records as narcotic users."

"Oh no," whispered Sylvia huskily, "not Lisa Gordon."

"No," he assured her, "not Lisa Gordon."

"Where does witchcraft enter into all this?" Edna's brows were furrowed and she was jiggling the ice in her glass.

Roberts sighed. "That's for you to find out. We don't know. Everything I've just told you is complete supposition. There's even a theory put forward that somehow the smuggling of foreigners into this country may be tied up to this business in some way. Thousands of Pakistanis and Indians enter this country illegally every year."

Sylvia held in reserve a comment she was about to make on British hospitality. Instead she said, "And somehow you think there's a connection with this *mishegoss*—excuse me, that more or less means nonsense, not that it is such—and Astoroth House."

"Everything is a possibility."

His obliquesness nettled Sylvia. Then she decided there was probably some British law that prevented him from committing himself outright, like the strict laws about libel. Anyway, he was charming and had succored Max in his hour of need. *Max!* She inquired eagerly, "Is he living in a nice room? Are there fresh bedsheets? No bedbugs in the mattress? Did he eat today?"

"Max is busy holding up his end."

Sylvia was about to respond that she wasn't interested in a physical description but thought better of it. Instead she asked, "How's Gypsy Marie? Is her cover holding up?" Sylvia took unrestrained pride in her knowledge of police jargon, thanks to Van Larsen's tutoring.

"Quite satisfactory. One of her homing pigeons arrived only an hour ago." He stared at a trouser leg, noticed a pinfeather and flicked it away. "It was molting. But the message in the capsule attached to the band around its leg tells us she has been inside Astoroth amd met the housekeeper."

"Good old Gyp," said Edna cheerily.

"Ladies," said Roberts leaning forward with a new seriousness, "you are involved in a very serious business, a very dangerous business. Lisa Gordon has disappeared and Max was almost murdered. These people will stop at nothing to protect themselves. For all we know, Astoroth House may be a false lead, a dead end. It might be coincidental that Lisa disappeared from there and Max took ill there."

"Ill!" yelped Sylvia. "He was almost *in memoriam*!"

"I'm simply saying, take care, and do not jump to conclusions. Just watch, listen . . . and pray you're invited there this coming weekend." He added with his usual understatement as he reached for his drink, "That would help enormously. I myself plan some grouse shooting in that area."

"Oh?" oh'd Edna with interest, "is it open season?"

"On just about everything these days, dear lady, on just about everything. I have taken as much precaution as possible to see that you'll all be protected, but still . . . there's always the unexpected slip, isn't there."

Edna wondered if she booked the next plane back to New York, would Sylvia slip her a white feather?

"The boy is being transported to his mother tonight. Max reports the disguise is excellent though the boy is still reluctant. Tomorrow, Friday, Max travels to Punting-on-the-Thames as the weekend guest of the local vicar, Oscar Treble."

Sylvia inquired with anxiety, "Supposing we don't get asked to Astoroth House, what then?"

"Well, the area is always of interest to tourists and there's quite a charming inn. But— " he paused effectively to sip his drink, "I think you'll be asked to Astoroth House. Er . . . how would you put it . . . my money's on Madame Vilna? Yes, my money's on Madame Vilna."

CHAPTER
six

After Sylvia had refreshed his drink, Detective-Inspector Roberts launched into a thorough and precise physical descriptoin of Astoroth House and its permanent occupants. He added little to what the chauffeur Harry Sanders had already told them about Sir Vernon Mayhew and his misbegotten son, little Lord Carson, but Judith Sondergaard was something else, like an unexpected dessert served Christmastime at the poorhouse.

"So, she used to conduct tours abroad for teen-age school girls, eh." Edna was picking at a cuticle as though trying to dislodge a hidden grain of added information. "Did she always return with the group intact? I mean, was there a head count before they left."

"Her past is spotless," averred Roberts.

"Nobody's past is spotless," said Edna, "unless they've been living in a bath of detergent since birth. Does she take part in the witch rituals?"

"Oh yes. She's a priestess."

Sylvia interposed solemnly, "How widely abroad has Miss Sondergaard travelled?"

"You name it, she's been there—with the exception of the United States and Canada."

"That's more than interesting, isn't it."

"Again, it could be coincidental." Sylvia made a mental note never to ask Roberts for a phone number. She was afraid he would offer only an approximation.

"Now, I must take my departure," he said rising, "I'm meeting Max in a few hours and I've some last minute details to attend to at the Yard. Mind you now," he raised an index finger, "the watchword is caution."

Edna was reminded of the day she was sworn into the Girl Scouts and then resigned five minutes later when she found out it wasn't coeducational. Sylvia gave Roberts his bowler and saw him to the door.

"You'll see that Max has a good dinner, won't you? He's had a shaky blood count since the late unpleasantness."

Roberts gave her his assurance, waved goodbye to Edna, and left. Edna leaned back in her chair, stretched out, and contemplated the pompoms on her pumps.

"I have an ominous foreboding," she intoned darkly, and Sylvia expected a clap of thunder.

"If you're building up to maybe we should sleep in the same bed tonight the answer is No." Sylvia was stretching out on the couch, after lighting a cigarette. Edna reached over for the Scotch bottle, measured the remains with a practiced eye, and then refilled her glass.

"We'd better order more booze. This bottle's practically shot." An unhearing Sylvia was in another world.

"*Hey!*"

Sylvia sat up with a startled jerk. "What? What's the matter?"

"You looked catatonic. What's wrong?"

"What's wrong? What could be wrong? We're besieged by the press at the airport, a best friend's daughter is missing, my lover is almost murdered by an overdose of a mushroom drug, we're driven into London by a homicidal chauffeur, we're spending the weekend with a chorus line of witches, white slavery is rearing its ugly head again (generously basted with drugs), you have an ominous foreboding, and you ask me *what's wrong?* Really Edna, you are *de trop*."

The rehearsal (act two, scene three) had been occupying the better part of the hour following Sir Leonard Greystoke's demise and Madame Vilna was still finding it difficult to concentrate. Her private thoughts persisted in being far more dramatic and of greater consequence. She sat on the aisle in the middle of the stalls permitting Dylan to have his head, to grow more secure in his sudden stroke of good fortune, to feel his own way, and stumble as often as possible like an infant taking its first steps—to feel as safe and secure as the early bird tugging a stubborn worm out of the ground, while a clever tabby hidden in the bushes behind chose the right moment to pounce.

And for the occasional moment when she paid attention to the rough rehearsal, she found herself surprisingly impressed by his frequent, unsuspected flashes of brilliance. But mostly she had been occupied castigating herself for the seemingly cavalier attitude in which she had treated Greystoke's death. It had all been a performance, all in keeping with the attitudes she had subliminally taught the company to expect of her. Boorish, domineering, overbearing, everything she had learned during a very brief tenure as student with the Actor's Studio in New York.

Inwardly she wept for the dead man. She had fought ferociously against casting him, but Sir Leonard had been a tradition, and in England traditions are not casually swept aside. After a week of working with the old man, she was amazed to realize that on the stage he almost convinced her he was the youth Shakespeare had envisioned. Eventually they shared their private jokes and frequently lunched and traded memories.

Was is possible her earlier jocularity could have so been misinterpreted by the great actor as to cause his final heart attack? There had been other clashes of verbal violence and yet he had emerged unruffled. Why now? Why today? She resisted an urge to beat her breast and was grateful for the absence of a fireplace filled with dying embers or she would have been smearing ashes on her forehead.

" 'Let me be cruel, not unnatural . . .' "

Dylan would have been Vilna's original choice for the part. He was the first actor to excite her instinct at the auditions. She had recognized the sleeping genius lying drugged beneath the dissolute exterior.

" 'I will speak daggers to her, but use none.' "

I, too, spoke daggers, thought Vilna morosely, without intention of using them. Mine were gentle daggers, amusing daggers, but, unwittingly, they pierced Sir Leonard's heart. Could he not realize I was merely joking about eliminating the soliloquy? Maybe fiddle with it a little here and there, help find a few laughs in it, perhaps, but total excision? *Never.*

" 'My tongue and soul in this by hypocrites . . .' "

Ah! Shakespeare, ah! Billy dolling, how well you knew. Hypocrites indeed. How stylishly and with what chic a few in my immediate vicinity wear their cloaks of deception. Very little escaped me that weekend at Astoroth House, very little indeed, and perhaps *they know.* Let us hope they do. It is important that they do.

"How in my words somever she be shent . . ."

Shent? Oy, Billy boy, if you meant *rebuked* why didn't you write *rebuked*? You couldn't spell it? But by any other name it is still appropriate to how I have been treating myself this past hour. Rebuke.

" *'To give them seals never, my soul, consent!'* "

My soul bleeds but it is time to apply the styptic pencil. He is dead and that's that. Death comes very cheaply

78

these days. Riots. Nicaragua. Murder. On stage at the Old Avon. *Enough*.

"Enough!" Madame Vilna shouted. She pulled herself to her feet and rumbled down the aisle. "That was quite pleasant. Thank you, Dylan. Within the next week we shall work to make it powerful, titanic, and then charge it with a *soupcon* of electricity. That will be all for today. Tomorrow morning at eleven promptly and can someone direct me to the nearest synagogue? I would care to light a *yurtzeit*, a memorial to Sir Leonard . . . "

Her voice wavered and died and the massive body trembled and stopped fighting the tears that inundated her cheeks.

In the gypsy encampment at Punting-on-the-Thames, Gypsy Marie Rachmaninoff sat at a campfire on a wooden crate, puffing a corncob pipe, and listening to the strains of a balalaika from a nearby wagon. From the forest of trees that separated the camp and Astoroth House, she saw the head of the tribe emerging dragging his daughter behind him, he cursing in Hungarian and the girl screaming in English.

"How often have I told you, stay away from that accursed zoo, Esmeralda!" shouted Magyar the chief.

"I like to feed the animals!" she pleaded.

"One day they will feed you to the lions!"

"Nah, they won't! I ain't no Christian!"

"Bah, you headstrong teen-age nomad!" all this in Hungarian. Brutally, he flung her to the ground and she fell at Gypsy Marie's feet sobbing.

"There, there," cooed Gypsy Marie, stroking the girl's matted, unwashed, grease-streaked hair, "don't cry. Your father is right. There is danger at Astoroth House."

As her sobs abated, the young girl raised her head and watched her father stalking to the head wagon. Then she turned to Gypsy Marie with a wicked grin.

"It isn't just for the animals I go there."

"Oh ho!" said Gypsy Marie knowingly, "it is one of the zoo attendants that attract you perhaps? Certainly not the backward son of the family!"

"He ain't all *that* backward," said Esmeralda much too knowingly. "No, it's none of them. But sometimes . . ." she looked around to make sure there were no other gypsies within earshot, "sometimes I look in the windows and let me tell *you* . . . !"

Gypsy Marie removed the pipe from her mouth. "I'm waiting."

Esmeralda repositioned herself with her legs crossed. "I have seen the woman in black and the man of the house *together*."

"Why not?" said Marie with a shrug. "They live there."

Esmeralda giggled. "Oh, you *are* funny. I hope your hunchbacked daughter Salmonella is as funny as you are."

"She's a scream."

"If I were to tell my father Magyar, what I am about to tell you, he'd wash my mouth out with sheep-fat soap."

"I don't use the stuff so tell me."

Esmeralda whispered in Gypsy Marie's ear and when she was finished, Gypsy Marie said, "Whoopee."

"Oh yes! Oh yes! Sometimes, Lord Carson watches with me but all he ever says is 'Daddy naughty, shame, shame.' "

Marie grabbed the girls's hand. "You are sure it was the master of the house you saw with his mistress?"

"I have young eyes," came the haughty reply, "they do not deceive me. I have seen other things, too, but I won't tell you about them until you tell my fortune."

"I told you your fortune after lunch. What could be new in six hours?"

Esmeralda pouted. "What I told you was new, wasn't it?"

"What you saw was old, what you told was new. What else have you to tell me?"

"My fortune first."

"I'll tell you what I see right off the bat," said Gypsy Marie with irritation. "One of these days I'm going to bash your skull in."

In the Green Room at the Old Avon, Dame Augusta Mayhew and Dylan Wake watched as Lady Valerie Crawford unscrewed a flask. Madame Vilna sat on a chair holding a vial of smelling salts under her nose. Lady Valerie decanted some brandy into a paper cup and placed it in Vilna's other hand.

"Drink it, dear."

Vilna downed the brandy in one gulp and then flung the paper cup aside and handed the smelling salts to Dame Augusta. "What happened today will give nightmares to my nightmares." She looked up at the three. "You understand, of course, don't you, that my seemingly cavalier attitutde to Sir Leonard's sudden death was merely to maintain the morale of the company. Oh God, how that hideous moment brought back a sudden memory of my potion scene as Chyenka in *Fahr Vuss Nemst Du Nisht Eine Onderra Nummen*, which is perhaps more familiar to you as *Romeo and Juliet*. Mind you, I am not unfamiliar with death, but it never ceases to disturb me."

"'You're tired, dear," said Lady Valerie with a surprising gentleness, "you're driving yourself too hard."

Dame Augusta managed to refrain from adding bitterly, "And us."

"You need rest," continued Lady Valerie.

"Me old darlin. ' " Dylan was kneeling at her side like

a hopeful suitor, gently stroking Vilna's hands which were bunched together in her lap like a cluster of over-ripe bananas. "You ought to take a few days' break."

"Impossible. I have in my midst my beloved Sylvia and that Edna. I cannot abandon themselves to themselves."

"Then, by all means, bring them," chimed Lady Valerie as she and her aunt exchanged glances.

"Bring them where?" asked Vilna innocently.

"To Astoroth House for the weekend of course," said Dame Augusta generously.

"Oh, but you are too kind. You are much too kind. How I have looked forward to revisiting your lavish showplace under a happier circumstance than my previous stay there." She patted Dylan's head and he got to his feet like a happy puppy who'd just been rewarded wih a biscuit, while Vilna, with some effort, positioned herself into a fair approximation of Rodin's *Thinker*. "But, it is too much of an imposition. But— " she was erect again. "Undoubtedly Sylvia and Edna will be highly titillated by the frequently unorthodox amusement you provide comes midnight Saturday. They too, if I have not already informed you, have of late been dabbling their dainty fingers in the occult arts." She clasped her hands, shut her eyes, and her face became serene, as she liltingly said, "Ah! how brilliant I was a few flimsy decades past as *der shwartzer chaleryah* in *Tzvai Fahrlurrener Kinder*, which translated is the *witch* in *Hansel and Gretel*."

"It's no imposition whatsoever!" Lady Valerie might have been announcing the arrival of a train on track nine. "Dylan is coming, too, aren't you Dylan dear?"

"Well now, mavourneen, let me think. I'd been planning to do a bit of work on *Hamlet*."

Vilna waved a hand disdainfully. "Relax. He's been plenty worked over."

"Of course you're coming, Dylan," It was more a command from Dame Augusta then a request.

"No rehearsal Saturday!" announced Vilna. "How say you?"

"Thank God," muttered Dame Augusta.

"We can leave tomorrow evening!" beamed Vilna.

"Lovely", said Valerie, "I shall instruct Miss Sondergaard to expect us. Now Vilna dear, you are a boor and a martinet but in my restrained way I do bear some affection toward you. You must look after yourself and not take on so about Leonard's passing. Look at it this way, he's been called to heaven by the Great Casting Director in the Sky and is probably rehearsing some astral production of *King Lear* or something equally prosaic and mundane."

"Indeed? Then you acknowledge there is a God?"

"But of course we do, you dear sweet creature. Why else do we mock Him?"

"Mockery is frequently for those we admire, is it not?"

"Oh, it's all semantics!" roared Dame Augusta. "Me for an extremely dry martini on the rocks and the telly. Where are you off to, Valerie?"

"Nothing planned. Dylan . . . are you free for dinner?"

"Ah macushlah, sad to say, I'm already spoken for."

"Miss *Locke*?" The way she ground on the name she might have been gouging out an eye.

Vilna was in like a click-beetle. "No, darling creature toward whom I also bear an eyedrop of affection, he is joining a party constructed of yours truly, the boor and martinet—which has on occasion described the Gemini Twins—alongside our visitors from abroad and Mister Joseph Gordon. But do join us and we can kill a few birds with you *finalemente* meeting Edna and Sylvia. Do not remonstrate! Make no false but polite excuses! I insist! Seven sharp at Sylvia's suite at the Dorchester."

"Actually, I'd love to," acquisced Lady Valerie in a voice that was pure halvah, "I'm looking forward to meeting the ladies."

"Believe me, Lady Valerie, on their part it is, as we say back home, likewise, I'm sure." She was on her feet. "Now then, I shall get me to a synagogue and then go home and bathe and change and meet you promptly at the appointed hour." With a graceful wave of her hand as she headed for the door she whispered. *"A tout a l'heure!"* and was gone.

Dylan crossed to the door, slammed it shut, and turned on the women angrily. "You must be daft!"

"Indeed?" purred Lady Valerie, "the pot calling the kettle black? What now, *old darling*? What now that you're starring with the company? What now, this sudden financial windfall?"

"Nelly's pregnant. I need help. I can use the money."

"Tut, tut, tut," admonished Dame Augusta, "you *will* continue to lead young girls astray."

A trace of a smile played on Dylan's lip. "I'm sure the irony was unintentional, Dame Augusta."

Detective-Inspector Roberts learned of Sir Leonard Greystoke's sudden death when he returned to his office. He immediately dialed the coroner.

"That you, Chip old boy?" He smiled at the mouthpiece. "Chan here. I believe you have a fresh cadaver on ice in the filing room. Greystoke comma Sir Leonard." He listened and then replied warmly. "Yes, he was enchanting in *Smilin' Through*. But I say, Chip, there's no immediate family to object to an autopsy, is there?" He listened. "Check it out, will you. I'd like one done as soon as possible. What? No, nothing special. Routine really. It certainly won't inconvenience old Greystoke, will it? Ha, ha, ha."

He hung up and clicked a switch on his intercom. "Puck, old lad. I'll be leaving in about an hour. Should there be any inquiries as to my whereabouts, just say . . . I've gone to the dogs."

In his small but cluttered two-room flat in South Kensington, Dylan Wake uncapped a bottle of Guinness and sank into a rocking chair. He took a swig and rocked gently for a few moments, then leaned his head back and closed his eyes.

Well, old darlin', you've finally gotten there. The big time. The Old Avon. *Hamlet*. A star. Can you carry it off? Sure you can, old genius. Sure you can. this is what you've been waiting for, haven't you? All those years of rep companies and third-rate tours and small unrewarding parts in flicks and on the telly. You know you're better then the rest of them, better then McKellan and Irons and Bates and Pasco, they just struck it lucky sooner that's all.

His eyes flickered open and he stared across the table at a photograph of himself and an older man.

Poor sod, he thought to himself as he stared at the older man in the photograph. You believed in me long before any of the others did, and I betrayed you. How long's it been since I so cruelly threw you out of my life? Two years? Three years? Does it matter? Does it matter how many thousands you threw away trying to promote me in films? That I worked my seductive ass off to make you think I loved you because I saw your vulnerability and used it the way I'd use a sheet of toilet paper. Where are you now, old sod? Back in Ohio, or was it Iowa, privately printing those thin sappy volume of poems that you give away as gifts. Was I much of a dent in your bankroll? As much of a dent as I was in your heart? Do you ever think of me? Do you ever think of that awful night in Paris when I treated you like shit—the deal was settled to do a movie at last and I thought I had it made and didn't need you any longer? Do you? I do, you bloody bastard. It haunts me worse then the other betrayals.

You screamed it then. You screamed it loud and

hysterically after throwing that glass of champagne in my face.

You're a whore! You're a stinking little whore! You'll never make it.

He flung the bottle at the photograph and both crashed to the floor. Dylan leapt to his feet, fists clenched, face contorted with rage, eyes misting, screaming, "I'm making it now, damn you! I'm making it now!"

His hands flew up and covered his face and he stood for a minute attempting to control his trembling body.

Am I really? Does it matter?

Hamlet or no *Hamlet* . . . it's gone too far . . . it's too late . . . too late . . .

Madame Vilna sat in the woman's section of a nearby synagogue, with a shawl covering her bowed head, her fingers intertwined, softly chanting the prayer for the dead.

Goodbye, Leonard, and forgive me, old chap.

She sighed and raised her head. May there be no other prayers needed for the dead this season. I enter a valley of death this weekend, with beloved friends who could be in serious danger.

And unselfishly there is also myself to consider.

Do they know I know what I know, let alone what I suspect? True, I have transferred everything with my ingenious total recall to the charming Detective-Inspector Roberts—whose remarkable resemblance to the late and ever lamented Ronald Colman is without question uncanny but most endearing—and he in turn has referred the aforementioned to my beloved Max Van Larsen . . . but still . . . there will be danger.

What the hell, like everything in the past, I shall meet it head on.

She lowered her head and interlaced her fingers again.

86

This is by way of a P.S., Leonard departed darling. Should you run into some of my old friends and confreres, say a hello.

Amen.

There was a knock at Dylan's door. He retrieved the photograph and bottle from the floor with shaking hands and placed them on the table. The second knock was more insistent. He crossed to the door and opened it.

"You're just about the last person I want to see right now," he snarled.

CHAPTER
seven

Lady Valerie and Dame Augusta shared a taxi after leaving the Old Avon.

"What's bothering you?" Lady Valerie asked the pensive older woman.

"I could begin with my arthritis but that's the least of it." She held a small thin cigar between the thumb and index finger of her left hand and flicked ash into the tray in the door on her side. "We've been much too smugly confident of late, Valerie. We must beware lulling ourselves into a feeling of false security."

"We're amply protected."

"I believe the Captain of the *Lusitania* said those very words the day of the disaster."

"Would you rather go back to admitting tours through Astoroth House?"

"I'd sooner have a pedicure with sheep shears. There's no turning back, we're in too deep for that. But we must learn to exercise greater caution."

"I gather you're against this coming weekend."

"Not in the least." She flicked ash. "It's easier to cope with adversaries on home territory. We went too far with Van Larsen. That was a serious error."

"Short of murder, what was there to do? He found his way to the subterranean cellar and saw the shipment. He had to be given the drug. Should he remember when he recovers, it can all be attributed to the hallucinations. We made a pact with that Devil when we signed the agreement . . . murder is *out*."

"Thank God my husband Irving didn't survive to see the low estate into which we've fallen."

"It was Irving's low estate that left us in this low estate," said lady Valerie acerbically. "Although I dare say the old bugger would have enjoyed our Order of the Fallen Angels."

"No dear," said the old lady with a faraway look, "Irving was perverse but unimaginative. What are you planning for Saturday night?"

"I haven't given it much thought. Perhaps a cruci-fixion."

"Oh darling," groaned Dame Augusta, "we've had that three weeks in succession."

"The levitation bit?" suggested Lady Valerie hopefully.

Dame Augusta wrinkled her nose. "All that bother of setting up piano wire. And if there's a strong wind I start swinging, and you know what happens if I forget my seasick pills."

Lady Valerie snapped her fingers. "We haven't had a kabalistic rite in months!"

"Oh yes!" Dame Augusta laughed mirthlessly. "That should flatter our Miss Plotkin no end, the kabala having been written by the ancient Hebrews. What do we do for an encore?"

"Well, we could reenact one of the Orphic Mysteries. Sondergaard really throws herself into *that*."

"Oh darling, that takes longer than an evening at the Old Vic, and you know I like to be in bed by a reasonable hour. Besides which, the faun comes down with colic after a session sucking at her breast."

Their taxi was now cruising through Mayfair along Curzon Street and Lady Valerie was longing for a brief soak in a hot tub. She snapped open her crocodile bag and rummaged for her change purse. "Let's not worry ourselves with it now. We've a few days in which to think. If worse comes to worse, we can always improvise. As a matter of fact, it might be wiser to wait and see how the weekend shapes up before finalizing the entertainment."

"I suppose you're right. Now, what about Nelly Locke?"

"What about her?" With a finger Lady Valerie was sorting coins in the change purse.

"The pregnancy."

"I must say they *are* getting a bit out of hand. This makes four in the past seven months."

"She's getting to be quite an expense." Dame Augusta lowered the door window and flipped the cigar butt out. "Himself is getting a bit bored with it, and I must say, I'm beginning to find it equally tiresome. I think it's time we had her up for the weekend."

Valerie sank back and pondered the old lady's suggestion. "It could be a bit tricky."

Dame Augusta was straining to push the window back up again. "Her pregnancies are getting out of hand. Sharing that flat with Lisa, she knows much too much. Why, at the rate she's going . . . bloody window . . . she might even demand you step aside and let *her* play Ophelia."

"She has to go."

"Quite." She examined the grease mark on her gloves left by the window projection and cursed the cab, the driver, and the company that owned and employed both.

"I'll give it some thought. Ah, I'm home." She pressed some coins into the older woman's hand. "My share."

"Thank you, dear. Have a nice time tonight. And Valerie . . ."

Valerie was in the street about to shut the cab door. "Yes, Gus?"

"Exercise great caution this evening."

"The ladies? I can handle them."

"Not so much the ladies, dear," said Dame Augusta as she reached over to pull the door shut, "Joseph Gordon." She pulled the door shut, rapped on the dividing glass between driver and passengers, and Valerie was left standing on the pavement with a quizzical expression on her face.

For a few seconds, Dame Augusta jiggled the coins in her hands as though she were about to cast dice, then opened her velvet purse and tossed them in. Her gray eyes stared out the window but saw nothing. She was thinking, what's a nice old octogenarian like me doing in a situation like this. Was there no other way out of our financial straits—short of taking in laundry? How subtly, how easily that Devil convinced us to join in his odious enterprise. Odious indeed, but comes the remuneration and they are most certainly all the perfumes of Arabia. But is it worth all this tension under which we live?

Yes.

I've nothing to lose. I'm an old woman. A very old woman. And old women are armored with selfishness. It's nice to have wealth again. It's nice to have my home to myself without making way twice weekly for hordes of the great unwashed, paying their two pounds to taste the fleeting thrill of a visit to a stately home.

She cackled softly to herself.

Stately home, indeed. There's bad blood in the Mayhews. There always has been. Irving and I were cousins which was certainly adding fuel to the fire. her eyes narrowed.

But they're getting close. That's not just arthritis I feel in my bones. They're getting close. Lisa Gordon, then Max Van Larsen and Nelly Locke, now Vilna and those two women from America. Witches indeed! Obviously misspelt.

I won't stand for murder, not anymore I won't. Irving might still be alive today if I'd known the true state of his insurance policy. A mere pittance, but then, he seemed to expire without pain.

The Old Devil just smiles and smiles and tells us we haven't a thing to worry about. He's right there in the thick of things and knows their every move. He assures us we can keep many jumps ahead of them. I'm too old to jump though the Devil knows I seem to be as graceful as a child at those rituals. Talk about your wonder drugs!

But I am uneasy. I am very uneasy. Seeing Sir Leonard lying there I couldn't help thinking, my time is running out, too. There's not much sand left in my portion of the glass. What about Valerie and Vernon and sad little Carson? Oh well, they keep insisting Satan looks after his own.

I hope there's a good movie on the telly tonight, not one of those scary horror films. They frighten me.

Lady Valerie entered the lobby of her apartment house and saw a familiar and impatient figure sitting in an armchair near the elevator.

"Saint Nicholas, darling!" she piped merrily, "what a pleasant surprise."

Nick Hastings pushed back his thinning blond hair, blinked his laser-beam blue eyes and followed his pointed nose to the oncoming beauty. He took her arm tightly and steered her to the elevator, speaking softly but crisply as they walked.

"What happened to Greystoke?"

"Dead, darling. Why?"

His finger poked the elevator button as he spoke out of the side of his mouth. "An autopsy's been ordered."

"So?"

"By Channing Roberts."

"Ah so."

The elevator appeared, and opened, and swallowed the two. As it ascended, Nick Hastings said, "My informant at the Yard doesn't like the look of it?"

"Why?" she asked with wide-eyed innocence.

"Autopsies are rarely performed on old men with known heart conditions. Would anyone have any reason to kill him?"

."Only the critics."

"On the other hand, Roberts may have ordered the autopsy merely to worry us."

"Nothing worries me, dear, you know that. I haven't worried since Vernon stopped sharing my bed. Coming for the weekend, dear?"

The elevator doors parted. The reporter led the way to the door of Lady Valerie's apartment.

"I wouldn't miss it for the world," said Hastings in reply to her question.

As Lady Valerie inserted the key in the lock she said, "By the by, Nelly Locke is becoming a bit of a nuisance."

"Pregnant again?"

"It could be authentic this time. She's been seeing Dylan again, the little beast. Shut the door and pour yourself a drink."

"None for you?"

"No dear. Need a clear head tonight." She told him of her invitation for the evening.

"I gave Evelyn Blair a lift back from the airport." He was pressing down on the syphon bottle.

"I *loathe* that woman," Valerie shouting from the bathroom where she was running the tub.

"She's a very clever newshen. I think she's on to something. The drive to London was one long third degree."

Valerie entered wearing a negligee. "Face it, she was almost like a mother to Lisa Gordon—even though Joe would never make it legal." She sat on a straightback chair and found a cigarette in a box on the coffee table in front of her. "Exactly what *does* she suspect?"

"She thinks Lisa's been spirited out of the country."

"Hmmmmm." She was lighting the cigarette.

"I think the Yard is on that wave-length, too."

"Well, we can't stop people from having their suspicions, can we?"

Hastings jiggled the ice in his glass. "They're coming dangerously close."

Valerie crossed her legs and exhaled a perfect smoke ring. "They were bound to sooner or later. But we're beautifully protected darling, aren't we? I mean if all this erupts into melodrama, Plan X goes into effect. Oh, don't you just love that? *Plan X.* It's like being a living part of one of those thrillers by Elsie Lee Mackintosh. Which reminds me. *Must* invite the vicar for dinner Saturday night."

"You're outrageous!"

She grinned roguishly. "That's part of my attraction, darling, isn't it?" She glanced at the desk clock. "Oh dearie me, I've so little time. But what the hell. Come on, dear. Let's take a bath."

Madame Vilna swept through the revolving doors of the Dorchester Hotel and the lobby lit up. She wore a matching gold lamé trouser suit under her black satin paillette-embroidered opera cape. Diamond-studded combs (paste) were artfully stuck in her jet black bun, and around her head was casually wrapped a lace mantilla, glowing with ruby and amethyst sequins. She commandeered the desk clerk who immediately informed Sylvia Plotkin one of her guests was ascending.

Sylvia stood anxiously in the hallway outside her suite until the elevator doors opened and Madame Vilna emerged with arms outstretched and weeping for joy.

"Sweet Sylvia!"

"Valiant Vilna!"

They fell into each other's arms while Edna appeared in the doorway snapping a bracelet around a wrist. "I've got the news tuned in on the TV set. Come on, we don't want to miss you. How's the Madame?"

"Vilna has had a most hideous day! Most hideous! It compares only with my disastrous opening night when I starred in *Der Boychick Vuss Fleet Im Der Luft*, which is perhaps more recognizable to you as *Peter Pan*."

She headed straight for the whisky bottle and poured herself a stiff drink. After a swift gulp (against a television background of rioting in Belfast which was no match for her recital), she informed them of Greystoke's untimely death and their weekend invitation to Astoroth House.

"Brava!" cried Sylvia hands outstretched and applauding a morose Vilna, "I must inform Mr. Roberts at once!"

As Sylvia dialed Scotland Yard, Edna gave Vilna a quick rundown on their day.

"We have all been busy little bees," commented Vilna drily, "but somehow, there is a taste of vinegar in our honey." Edna, who was sitting next to Vilna on the couch, winced as a beefy palm connected mercilessly with her innocent and unsuspecting left knee. "So how many did you pinch today?" Sylvia crossed from the phone with her face a brown study.

"What's wrong?" asked Edna.

"He's gone to the dogs."

"I beg your pardon?"

"That's what they told me at the Yard. Roberts is out. He's gone to the dogs."

"Undoubtedly the greyhounds," elucidated Vilna.

"Where greyhounds?" asked Sylvia.

"White City. Every Thursday and Saturday nights, rain or shine and without fail, there is greyhound racing." She was struggling out of the cape. "I have had occasion twice to be taken there by young Dylan Wake. It is most amusing and once profitable. So your Detective-Inspector is a gambling man?"

Sylvia sat. "He has a rendezvous with Max."

Vilna's hands came together like a bowling ball making a ten strike. "You did not tell me on the phone he was here!"

"I couldn't. Joe Gordon was with us when you called."

"But of course. Very secret. Very cloak and dagger. It brings back pleasant memories of my tour in the old melodrama *Ich Ken Dir Gornisht Zuggen*, which is perhaps more familiar to you as *Secret Service*."

"*You're on!*" shrieked Edna and all heads swivelled towards the television set. There was Sylvia with Edna at her side being interrogated by Nick Hastings.

"Oh my God, I'm *fat*," yelped Sylvia.

"Hush!" hissed Vilna, "by me you are a sylph."

Edna preened. "Don't I photograph divinely? I wonder if I can buy a clip of this." Vilna glared and Edna's mouth clamped shut. Her eyes travelled to Sylvia who (with a somewhat unbelievable modesty) was staring at the floor. Edna leaned over and poked her. "Hey! You're missing yourself!"

"I've seen it all before," said Sylvia abstractedly.

Max. Greyhounds. White City. Greyhounds. Max. Max. Max.

Edna was wondering if all was well with Sylvia. She was positive the humming she was hearing was *Somewhere I'll Find You*.

Dylan Wake's hand connected with Nelly Locke's cheek and she screamed. "I told you never to come here again," he shouted. "We're finished!" He struck her again and Nelly reeled backward, falling against the door. "You're not going to screw up my big chance, not this one you aren't."

Her eyes were astonishingly tearless. Her face was an asbestos sheet and her lips were curled in a sneer usually reserved for the advances of unattractive casting directors. "I'm having dinner tonight with Evelyn Blair." Each word struck him like pellets from a pea-shooter.

Dylan's shoulders sagged. He shook his head sadly, folded his arms and turned his back on her. "I can't get the money tonight," he said in a strangled voice. "There's no time."

"Make the time!"

He spun around angrily. "The banks are closed! Neither one of them carries this much cash on them!"

"A piece of jewelry will do," she said coldly.

"You're daft. Oh Christ, how you are daft!" He was pacing the room running one hand frantically through his red hair. "You *are* asking for trouble. Oh *Christ*, how you are asking for trouble!" With his hands he propped himself against the table. "You keep this up and they'll do you! They will *do* you."

"The *ladies*?" came the pointedly snide inquiry.

"You know who I'm talking about. Lisa told you enough. Not everything. But enough." A finger shot forward pointing ominously at Nelly. "You watch your step tonight, you little bitch. You be careful what you say to that reporter. You'll have the money tomorrow and that had better be the end of it."

"I'm not afraid of you or them." With one hand she smoothed the front of her dress and then said quietly, "I want to marry you." Dylan was momentarily transfixed. "You're going to make it now and I want my share. I saw you through those lean years after you threw your sugar daddy over in Paris."

"Nobody's riding in on my coattails," he rasped.

"Think about it. It makes sense. You'll need a change of image now. You've been a parasite long enough. And I've got all the strength the two of us need."

"No contest there," admitted Dylan with a strange smile. "None whatsoever. Now, get the hell out of here." Each stared at the other with defiance for a few moments and then Nelly blew him a mocking kiss, groped for the knob, opened the door, and left.

"Jesus wept," whispered Dylan to the door, "Jesus indeed wept." He shook cobwebs from his head and crossed to a wall mirror. "Ah me old darlin', your pigeons are coming home to roost!" he was unbuttoning his shirt. "And I love, I simply love pigeon pie."

He leaned over and gently kissed his reflection.

Although it was still an hour until the first race, the thirteen-shilling compound at White City was crowded with early diners and drinkers. They stood at the two bars in either section of the large and comfortable lounge or ate at tables or the counter that ran half the length of a wall just past the entrance betting booths. The green light in each cage of the betting booths would light and signal the start of bets acceptable until fifteen minutes before the first race. There was a subdued hum of voices as selections were compared and tips traded.

In a secluded corner of the inside lounge, Detective-Inspector Roberts shared a couch with Max Van Larsen, his priestly garb complete with thick glasses and hat drawing an occasional astonished or bemused glance from the White City regulars. Both men held a beer and a sandwich and were deep in hushed conversation. An hour earlier, Max had transferred the responsibility of Quasimodo-Salmonella to the yard detective who would be delivering Quasi to his mother at midnight. Max tugged at his clerical collar. Beyond Roberts, through a wall of sheet glass that contained a swinging glass door at each side, Max could see the grandstands, the track, and the betting board erected at the far side of the oval.

"Nervous?" asked Roberts with amusement.

"I don't think they often get to see a priest in this place."

"They don't expect them in brothels either, but they show up."

"I've never done the disguise bit before. I keep expecting at any moment to be recognized."

"By whom? Lady Valerie's set doesn't patronize this place. I thought it was a charming idea on my part to select this place. And besides, I've got a couple of hot tips."

Out of the corner of his eye, he recognized one of his detectives, Arthur Simmons, scanning the enclosure.

"That's one of my men," Roberts told Max as he indicated with his head. Simmons spotted Roberts and walked leisurely towards him. He greeted Roberts like a long-lost friend, was introduced to "Father Green," and as the men made room for him on the couch, took his cue, and sat while removing his hat. He kept a fixed smile as he spoke.

"I have the autopsy report on Greystoke."

"Ah! Good!" Roberts took a swig of beer.

"He had a fatal dose of cucumber juice."

Roberts choked and went red. Simmons gently patted his back.

"What kind of a joke is that!" demanded Roberts when his choking fit had ended.

Simmons sighed. "I had the same reaction when Chip told me." He reached into his inside jacket pocket and found a slip of paper. He handed it to Roberts who read the two words carefully printed in red ink:

Ecballium elaterium.

Roberts passed the slip of paper to Max who admired the neat script and then looked appropriately puzzled.

Simmons elucidated. "The squirting cucumber. Its seeds and juice are poisonous. Grows primarily in tropical or semitropical climates. Apparently its skin is so delicate, that when brushed by a passer-by, it ejects its seeds and a stream of poisonous juice that stings the skin. That can sometimes be fatal if it enters the pores. Taken orally, it's always fatal."

"That's a new one on me," said Max.

"Move over," added Roberts glumly. "Greystoke obviously got it orally, unless they've got a hothouse at the Old Avon."

"There's one at Astoroth House," said Max.

"Dear, dear, dear," murmured Roberts. "Now why Greystoke? He's figured nowhere in our investigations."

Max leaned across Simmons. "He was with the Old Avon. Likewise Dame Augusta and Lady Valerie."

Roberts nodded and folded his hands together. "Damn, the one thing I want to avoid is this sort of kafuffle."

"Then avoid it," said Max.

"What?"

"I said avoid it. Until, let's say, Monday."

"Ah! *Ah!*" Had a dentist been hovering over Roberts' open mouth at that moment, it might have been love at first sight.

Max continued talking in a low voice, and what he said was only heard by his two companions and from the way Roberts kept nodding his head eagerly, at least a dozen people at nearby tables were aching to hear the tips they presumed were being passed.

Oscar Treble sat on a stone bench in the pleasant, well-tended garden behind the vicarage at Punting-on-the-Thames. His hands loosely held a six-red panpipe into which he was blowing with an airy savoir-faire that brought an occasional lyrical response from a lonesome oriole perched on a branch overhead. Oscar Treble when standing measured an economical though compact five feet and his rosy, cherubic countenance belied his sixty years. He bounced merrily like a bobbin at the end of a fishing line and the occasional passer-by choosing to stand on tiptoe and peer over the hedge that separated the garden from the sidewalk beamed with amusement and pleasure at the puckish man they had inherited some two years earlier. Mr. Treble's predecessor, an acne-scarred man in his forties, had absconded to the continent with a choirboy and it was rumored they were enjoying an unusual success touring cabarets with a Laurel and Hardy act.

"Vicar!"

Mr. Treble lowered the pipe, cocked his head, and squinted in the direction of an open door that led to the vicarage kitchen. Into focus came the round figure of his housekeeper, Amanda Brush, looking anxiously into the garden while she dried her hands on the calico apron tied about her ample waist.

"Din-dins ready!" trilled Amanda Brush.

Din-dins, thought the vicar with distaste. Miss Brush's occasional lapses into baby-talk were attributable to a previous tenure as nursemaid to a trio of unmanageable monsters who had almost succeeded in burning her at the stake during an orgy of Cowboys and Indians.

"Coming, Amanda," said the vicar amenably.

Amanda Brush returned to the stove, lifted the cover of a kettle, and vigorously stirred the cock-a-leekie soup which had three times come to a boil. The vicar bounced into the room and placed the pipe on the kitchen table. "I shall dine in the study tonight, Amanda."

Amanda straightened up and spoke as she re-covered the kettle, "But the table's set in the dining room."

"The study, Amanda," said the vicar as though attempting to nail every word to her ear, "I must complete a chapter of my newest thriller this evening and I can work while I'm eating. I'm having unusual difficulty with Black Bernard."

Black Bernard was the protagonist of some twelve of the vicar's novels written under the pseudonym of Elsie Lee Mackintosh.

"Black Bernard is trapped in Iran and I'm having some difficulty extricating him for the trip to Lebanon. I sometimes wish I was more adroit at foreign intrigue." He stood at the kitchen table with fingertips pressed together studying Miss Brush's ample posterior as she now bent and basted a small lamb roast in the oven. "Oh, for the good old days when readers were content with missing wills and mistaken identities. But alas, in these violent times, they demand meatier stuff. Still, I manage to keep up with the times, don't I, Amanda?"

Amanda shut the oven door and straightened up with a jagged smile. "You never cease to send chills up *my* spine, Mr. Treble."

The vicar returned her smile agreeably and then crossed to the door that led to his study, the far wall of which was covered with a huge map of the world into which myriads of varicolored pins were stuck. The vicar crossed to the map and studied the area separating Iran from Lebanon. Deep in thought he stroked his fleshy chin as Miss Brush entered carrying a place setting which she proceeded to lay out carefully on his desk.

"Dame Augusta phoned while you were out," she reminded herself to tell him. The vicar's shoulders heaved as he laughed silently. The silent laugh was a triumphant one as he found a solution to Black Bernard's predicament and moved a pin. "Dinner at eight Saturday night. She promises a most provocative evening."

The self-satisfied vicar moved away from the map rubbing his hands together. "I suppose she wants to borrow you for the evening to assist with the service."

"I wouldn't miss it for the world," said Miss Brush gleefully.

"Well, lay off the port," warned the vicar sternly, "I don't relish the sight of you cavorting around their garden on a broomstick again. It's most unbecoming at your age."

"Whoosh!" said Miss Brush with a snort. "Is it any worse than *yourself* hobnobbing with those who bare their tongues and their backsides at the Almighty?"

The vicar's eyes rolled and showed white. "How often must I remind you, Amanda, the bacchanalian revels at Astoroth House are mere whimsy and hardly to be taken seriously. In these permissive times one must take the broader view. I'm not one of those hellfire and brimstone preachers. I'm *au courant*! That explains my unusual popularity among the parishioners. Ergo, I strive to make my sermons wry, dry, and slyly witty. I'm sure the Lord is very pleased every Sunday to hear the uproarious response to my occasional boffola. Does Dame Augusta wish me to return her call?"

"At your convenience," said Miss Brush as she waddled back to the kitchen.

The vicar sat at his desk, pushed his writing pad aside, and reached for the telephone. As he waited to be connected with Dame Augusta's London number, he leaned back and repositioned his swivel chair in order to study the map on the wall again.

"Yes, yes," he muttered to himself, "that's the only route for Black Bernard this time. Hello? Hello? Augusta? Are you well, my dear? Oh, I'm super! Now then my dear, what's on the menu for Saturday?" He listened for a few moments and then emitted a roar of laughter. "Oh, by the by, my dear, I might have a guest staying with me this weekend. Hmm? A young Canadian priest, a Father Green, I believe. He's the friend of a friend, but then, we're all cut from the same cloth, aren't we? Ha, ha, ha, ha, ha. What? You are too kind, Augusta. Much too kind."

Amanda Brush was entering with a loaded tray.

"Of course, it's all right for Amanda. Yes, she is turning into a mad maenad! Ha! ha!"

"What's a maenad?" growled Amanda.

The vicar covered the telephone mouthpiece with his hand and hissed, "A nymph!"

Miss Brush smiled with contentment and placed a bowl of soup in front of the vicar.

Tears were stinging Nelly Locke's cheeks as she left Dylan Wake's building. She brushed angrily at her eyes as she headed for Kensington High Street and the cul-de-sac five streets north where she'd been sharing the flat with Lisa Gordon.

Stinking weakling, she thought to herself still dwelling on Dylan, stinking little coward. She was recalling a day a year earlier when Dylan had received a telegram from his mother who lived in Blackpool informing him his father was dead.

"He's dead, oh my God, he's dead," moaned Dylan through the fingers of the hands covering his face, "now I'm the head of the family. Oh my God, I don't want to be the head of the family." And then the swiftness with which his hands fell away from his face as an idea clicked. "I know what I'll make mum do. I'll make her turn the flat into digs for touring actors. Then she can support herself!"

Stinking weakling. Nelly was now in the saloon bar of a pub ordering a double gin and tonic. She counted out the exact amount of coins, laid them on the counter, and perched on a stool.

Bloody weakling. How often had it been up to me to pay the rent when I lived with him. You've a short memory, my lad, but not Nelly. Nelly remembers everything. She has a large file in her head with an invisible time-lock attachment. And when the time-lock goes off, thought Nelly grimly as the barmaid placed her order in front of her, the file will spring open and its contents will spill over into appropriate laps unless I get what's due me!

She sloshed tonic into the glass holding the gin, stirred it with her index finger, and drank as though she'd been wandering lost in a desert for a week.

Fifteen minutes later she was back on the High Street heading towards the cul-de-sac, the gin and tonic unsuccessful in dousing her fire of inner rage. She glanced at her wristwatch and realized there was only a half hour until Evelyn Blair would be coming by for a drink. She hugged the pint of whisky she'd bought at the pub to her chest and turned into the narrow mews street, in her right hand the key ready to be inserted into the downstairs lock.

In a few moments, she was climbing the cramped staircase to the third floor, her lips moving in silent hatred. Her legs ached slightly as they always did when she reached the door to her flat, unlocked it and entered. She clicked the switch at the right of the door as she entered and then let out a guttural croak as something of intense weight struck the base of her skull. Her knees crumpled and her body sagged as she dropped the whisky bottle to the floor.

She fell face downward, semiconscious. Before she completely blacked out she wondered, was my performance really that bad? Really all that bad? Why then the hissing?

CHAPTER
eight

Dylan Wake entered the elevator at the Dorchester and found a smile for Lady Valerie Crawford whose emerald green dress smartly showcased her shapely legs. She was examining her pretty face in her compact mirror when she heard Dylan say, "I see we're both fashionably late." It was ten minutes past seven.

"I was watching Miss Plotkin on the news," said Lady Valerie as she snapped the compact shut and popped it back into her silver lamé purse. "I must say, she wasn't exactly what I expected from Max's description. Struck me as a bit dowdy. Good heavens, you're wearing a clean shirt and a suit. But of course, you're *starring* at the Old Avon now, aren't you?"

The elevator operator sneaked a quick glance at Dylan and was unimpressed.

"What kept *you*, Dylan? You're usually so prompt for free drinks and free dinner."

Dylan explained with a familiar insinuation, "Nelly dropped in on me unexpectedly."

"Oh, isn't that a coincidence! Augusta and I were thinking earlier we might ask her up for the weekend."

"I think that's a charming idea."

"I thought you would." Valerie's smile reflected porcelain.

The elevator doors parted and Dylan heard laughter. His eyes darted to the right and espied the open door to Sylvia and Edna's suite. "Ah!" ah'd Dylan, "the revels have begun." He took Valerie's hand. "May I lead the way?"

"Of course. You so rarely do."

Joseph Gordon was the first to espy the new arrivals. "Here they are! My God Val, green does wonders for you!"

Sylvia Plotkin took one look at Valerie Crawford and felt like Bette Milder. Edna St. Thomas Shelley took one look at the grinning Dylan Wake and decided he was undernourished and oversexed. Sylvia crossed to them with hands outstretched. "How nice to meet you both! I'm Max Van Larsen's Sylvia!" She lurched forward as Dylan grabbed her hand.

"Who is Sylvia and what is she?" he murmured seductively and then planted a kiss on her hand.

Sylvia jocularly clutched her heart and turned to Edna. "They know how to treat a lady in this country." Dylan released her hand and she smiled at Lady Valerie. "I've heard sooooo much about you!"

"It's all true my dear, every word of it! I saw you on the news and you were absolutely enchanting!"

Joe Gordon poured drinks while Madame Vilna introduced Dylan and Valerie to Edna. Valerie smiled at her hostesses. "I gather we're sisters under the skin."

Edna played with the round silver locket that hung from a chain around her neck. "I carry my evil neutralizer in this."

Valerie admired locket and chain. "How very wise of you, Edna. And so much more becoming then the ordinary necklace of garlic."

"Joe Gordon held two drinks. He gave one to Valerie.

"Your usual my dear. Vodka and two drops of absinthe."

"How sweet of you to remember."

Joe crossed to Dylan with the remaining drink. "Whisky and water, Dylan."

"Thanks, me old darlin'." Joe's clenched fists went unnoticed by all except Madame Vilna.

"I can hardly believe we're in England at last," said Edna airily. "Our first trip!"

"What took you so long to get here?" asked Lady Valerie.

"We swam," tromboned Edna.

Lady Valerie retreated to Sylvia. "You *will* be joining us at Astoroth House this weekend, won't you!"

"I wouldn't miss it for the world! You're an absolute darling to ask us! Imagine! One of the most famous homes in England and *we'll* be spending the weekend there! You know, I'm not only Jewish, I'm an Anglophile. I gather we leave tomorrow night after your rehearsal."

Joseph Gordon interjected swiftly. "Now, if I were on that invitation list, we could all up in my car!"

Lady Valerie nimbly picked up the cue. "You know you have a standing invitation, Joe."

"Now, aren't I the brazen one?" said Gordon and then laughed. There was five minutes of amiable chatter while Edna sniffed around Dylan Wake as though he was an antique pomander dangling around the neck of an eighteenth-century courtesan. Lady Valerie and Sylvia had their heads together with Sylvia assuring the beauty that Max was well out of danger. Madame Vilna held Joe Gordon in a conversational headlock learning little more about his daughter's disappearance. Dylan was regaling Edna with his amazing good luck at replacing the late Leonard Greystoke as Hamlet, and Edna asked Dylan if there was any hope of their changing the ending.

"I always feel after Horatio's done that 'Good night, sweet prince' crap," said Edna, "Hamlet should open his eyes, fling his arms around Horatio's neck, kiss him on the lips and scream 'Surprise!' "

"For God's sake, don't tell Vilna," cautioned Dylan with twinkling eyes. "With 'How all occasions do inform against me' she has me doing a time-step."

"Everybody! Everybody!" It was Gordon in the center of the room demanding their attention. "Drink up! It's time to get the show on the road!"

"Urmph," said Dylan.

Sylvia was all wide eyes. "Where are you taking us?"

"A little surprise I've planned!" said the beaming Gordon, "we're going greyhound racing!"

Sylvia went white and found Edna's eyes. Edna returned her anxious glance with a shrug.

"One of my dogs is racing tonight." Gordon informed the, "and I need you all there for good lock."

"Oh, which one?" trilled Lady Valerie.

"Witches Brew in the third," said Joe with a smile. "She's looking mighty good lately. Ran her in the trials yesterday and she beat five tough runners by a nose!"

Max, thought Sylvia attempting to quell a small inner panic, what happens if Max is still there and he's recognized? Should I excuse myself, run to the bedroom, phone White City, and page Channing Roberts? Or the devil take the hindmost?

The Devil.

Witches' Brew.

Sylvia shuddered.

"Cold, dear?" inquired Lady Valerie who had twice played nursing sisters on television.

Sylvia managed a smile. "I guess somebody walked over my grave."

"And where's that?"

Sylvia decided she ought to laugh and did and heard Dylan shouting to Joe, "I've got ten shillings riding on your dog!"

Gordon ignored him. "The car's downstairs. Come on everybody, chop chop! It's a fifteen minute drive and the first race is at seven forty-five!"

Madame Vilna was entertaining thoughts of her own as how to possibly rescue them from the situation—such as throwing herself from the window—but dismissed that due to her morbid fear of heights. "Oh well," she trumpeted instead, "as I said at the final curtain of *Oy Vuss Hayser Zochen Follen Frum Der Himmel*, which is perhaps more familiar to you as *The Last Days Of Pompeii*, 'We who are about to die salute you.' "

"How utterly droll," said Lady Valerie as she swept towards the door which Gordon was holding open. Sylvia sidled over to Edna.

"What do we do? What do we do? I'm positive that's where Roberts is meeting Max!"

"It's probably *very* crowded there," suggested Edna in a weak attempt to allay Sylvia's fears which she privately shared, "running into them is unlikely."

Evelyn Blair, a vision in heavy checked tweeds, rapped on the door again.

"Nelly! Nelly? It's Evelyn *Blair*!" she blared. She tried rattling the doorknob. then she pressed her ear to the door and smelled the unpleasant odor of gas.

"Nelly!" she shouted. Then she sniffed again and rushed to the door of the opposite apartment, banging ferociously, and shouting, "I say in there, are you home? Help! Gas! Help!"

Dylan Wake was the last to enter the Rolls Royce. He stared hard at Harry Sanders who held the door open and whispered, "How's me old darlin'?"

Harry's lips formed two words and Dylan didn't have to be a lip reader to know he was being told to do something he'd been told to do on many previous occasions. Dylan snickered and bent to enter the car. Harry resisted the urge to help him in with his right foot. The door slammed shut as Dylan settled into a jump seat next to Joe Gordon and Edna. Valerie sat opposite him next to Vilna and Sylvia.

"Don't spare the horses!" shouted Joe as Harry got in behind the wheel.

"I thought we were going to the dogs," said Sylvia weakly.

"You'll love it, darlin'," said Dylan, "you can bet as little as two shillings, you know."

"We won't stay for the entire card if you get hungry," said Gordon. "We can leave anytime after we've cheered my Witches' Brew to the finishing line."

"First, of course," caroled Lady Valerie. She turned to Edna, as Harry pulled into the Park Lane traffic. "How long have you been indulging in witchcraft, dear?"

"Seems like aeons," retorted Edna swiftly. "It was just a dabble here and a dabble there until last summer when Sylvia and I were out on Long Island and got swept up into the East Hampton Daughters of Satan. We've never regretted it for a moment, have we, Syl?"

"It altered the course of our lives," Sylvia joined in glumly, "they're a fun bunch."

"Does your group believe in reincarnation?" asked Lady Valerie.

"Doesn't everybody's?" inquired Edna archly. "Everytime one of our girl's goes into a trance . . . you remember Tiger Ginsberg, Sylvia . . . she comes up Marie Antoinette and loses her head again." Edna leaned back smugly and then asked Lady Valerie, "Do you stick to a strict thirteen for your covens?"

"Oh heavens no! We don't go in for any Halloween type of mumbo jumbo. The attendance at our sabbaths vary."

Madame Vilna's head was spinning.

"Do you draw on the local village?" Edna might have

been a precocious college undergraduate preparing a term paper.

"Oh heavens yes! They throw themselves into it with gay abandon! Why even our vicar, Mr. Treble, participates."

"The vicar!" exclaimed Edna, "How does he explain it when he says his prayers?"

Lady Valerie laughed. "My dear, it's innocent fun, really."

"Our bunch takes it very seriously," intoned Edna. "They draw their practices from the late Aleister Crowley, not to mention a suggestion or two from the works of Sir Francis Dashwood of Hellfire Club fame. Next season we're planning our own production of Marlow's *Doctor Faustus*." Edna was grateful now that Sylvia had forced her through their one week crash course in the reference room at the New York Public Library.

The Rolls emerged from Hyde Park and turned into Bayswater Road.

"Traffic's heavy," commented Gordon, "it's going to be a big night at White City. Yup, look's like a big crowd tonight."

Color came back to Sylvia's face as Gordon's words made her hopes soar. Everyone in the car knew Max Van Larsen. If he was to be recognized, the entire venture would collapse. They might never learn why Lisa disappeared or who tried to kill Max and what the true secret of Astoroth House was. And Sylvia loathed failure.

"Did you hear that, Syl? There's going to be a big crowd tonight." Edna's face was a map of reassurance.

"Oh yes," said Sylvia, "the more the merrier!"

Evelyn Blair sat in the back of the ambulance staring at Nelly Locke's white face. The ambulance attendant (still winded from applying the kiss of life) was giving the prone figure an injection.

"Oh, why should a child like this attempt to take her own life?" wailed Miss Blair, inwardly anxious to get to a phone and relay the story to the city desk.

The ambulance attendant said nothing. He kept to himself the bruises he had located at the base of Nelly's skull.

Evelyn Blair hoped she was giving an award-winning performance of a distraught friend. She didn't for one minute think Nelly had attempted to kill herself. She was positive this was a desperate attempt to forever still her tongue.

She knows too much. Much too much. Was she stupid enough to tell somebody she was having dinner with me?

I wonder. I do indeed wonder.

"Will she pull through?"

The ambulance attendant wondered why she didn't have the nodes of her vocal chords removed. She sounded like a buzz saw going though steel.

"She's in very bad shape," he said with a cockney twang.

Evelyn wondered why he didn't have his adenoids attended to.

"Could you give me some odds?" she pleaded. "Like maybe fifty-fifty?"

The attendant shook his head. "Not even that good, I don't think."

Miss Blair's shoulders sagged. Nelly was her last hope. Her very last hope. She had no other leads short of attempting to storm Astoroth House, and three previous attempts had met with failure.

"Do your damndest," she rasped, "do your damndest. I can get your picture in the paper."

The first race at White City was about to begin and the thirteen-shilling enclosure was jammed. Joseph Gordon and entourage pushed their way past the betting windows to the rear lounge. Sylvia's eyes search the crowd for a priest and luckily for the moment she couldn't find one.

Edna hissed in her ear, "Maybe they left."

Madame Vilna was marvelling aloud at the large numbers of Chinese, Hindus, and Pakistanis present.

"Oh, they're very big gamblers," Dylan informed her. "They spend hours doping the dogs."

"The villains!" boomed Vilna.

"No, no, no, old darlin'," cautioned Dylan, "not *that* kind of doping . . . figuring out the possible winners!"

"Aha!" Vilna was glowing. "How I adore mingling with the masses of all races, creeds, and colors! Perhaps if there was more greyhound racing in America, there would be less racial strife!" She leaned over to a nearby Chinese. "You got a hot tip for a cold Russian?"

The startled man fled.

Lady Valerie found a sachet in her purse and held it to her nose.

A bell rang. There was shoving and jostling as part of the crowd attempted to elbow their way outside to watch the race. Dylan had made it to a betting window in time to lay ten shillings on the favorite, Clumsy Clovis. He elbowed his way back to Sylvia and grabbed her hand. "Come on outside! Ever see a dog race before?"

"No!" shouted Sylvia over the din.

"You'll love it! They're wonderful! Mean little buggers, too! They jostle and shove each other as though they had jockeys on their backs!" He had successfully maneuvered them outdoors and Sylvia's heart stood still.

She saw a priest.

The crowd roared as the lights dimmed. At the given signal the electric rabbit began hurtling around the circumference of the track toward the dogs shrilly yelping in the six-compartment oblong cage set in the center of the track. The rabbit reached the cage, the traps were sprung, and swift as lightning six dogs went tearing in pursuit.

The priest turned to a companion and Sylvia sighed with relief. It was not Van Larsen.

It was now the twenty-minute interval before the start of the third race. Dylan and Madame Vilna were elated at having chosen two winners so far, while Lady Valerie was feeling hunger pangs. Gordon and Edna were at the bar and Sylvia had gone to the ladies' room to powder her nose. In addition to worrying about encountering Max and the Detective-Inspector, she was trying to sort out certain questions that had been subtly gnawing at her brain for the past half hour.

Certain words were dancing a barcarole in her head. Rolls Royce. Chauffeur. Witches' Brew. Exactly how much does a foreign correspondent earn?

"Sanctuary," a familiar voice whispered in her ear. Sylvia turned and nodded in agreement to Lady Valerie.

"I never thought I'd have to go to a ladies' room for air," said Sylvia. "We don't have much time before the third race, do we?"

"Oh about ten minutes. Joe's certainly bet a bundle on his dog."

"Good heavens! Can he afford it?"

"What gambler can?" asked Valerie good-naturedly, and for a moment Sylvia thought she might like her. "You know Joe brought Max and myself here a few weeks ago. Maxie loved it."

Maxie!

"I didn't know," said Sylvia. "I'm afraid Max was not very lucid when we left."

"How sad," said Valerie. "We still can't figure out what came over him."

Sylvia took the plunge. "I think it was something he ate."

116

Lady Valerie was at a mirror tidying her hair. She smiled at Sylvia's reflection. "Max was very tired and under a strain. Did you know he'd been drinking a great deal?"

"Maxie can hold his liquor," said Sylvia archly.

"Well whatever it was, it was a terrible thing to see. I'm sure Madame Vilna must have told you."

"Yes."

"I miss Max. I do hope I'll see him again."

"Yes."

"You're very much in love with him, aren't you?"

"He's the universe and I'm his satellite."

They were now facing each other. "How'd you get him to accept the witchcraft bit?"

"Max likes me to have hobbies."

"He was outspokenly anti when he was at Astoroth House."

"That's so unlike Max to be impolite."

"We did a crucifixion for him that Saturday night. I thought it went beautifully. Max was repelled." She might have been giving Judith Sondergaard the breakfast menu.

"Who was the victim?"

"Dylan."

Sylvia's eyes flew wider.

"*Simulated* crucifixion, darling. Now really, Sylvia. Of course, when the victim throws himself into it as avidly as Dylan does, it does seem a bit frightening to the uninitiated. You know I sometimes think Dylan's convinced he's Christ reincarnated. Oh how he writhed and screamed on the ankh."

"The *what*?"

"Oh? Don't you know about ancient Egyptian practices?"

"My bunch hasn't touched it yet. We're mostly Jewish."

"The ankh is the cross used by the ancient Egyptians, the *crux ansata*. It's said to contain the power of life."

117

"Isn't it a contradiction to use the power of life for crucifixions?"

"Isn't ours a sad world of contradictions?"

At last they'd found something they could agree on.

Fifteen minutes later, Sylvia and Lady Valerie joined their group in cheering Witches' Brew to an easy victory. Joseph Gordon waved his winning tickets jubilantly while an increasingly liquor-besotted Dylan Wake favored his with a kiss. Madame Vilna was fascinated by a young Pakistani (who looked like a brown dormouse sketched by Beatrix Potter), gazing past her with unmasked loathing. Vilna turned her head and decided Dylan Wake was the object of disaffection. She poked Dylan with her elbow, indicated the dormouse, and inquired, "Friend of yours?" Dylan focused on the young Pakistani and said nothing.

Joseph Gordon was attempting to lead the way inside to the pay window. The human buzzing and undertones surrounding Sylvia made her think she was trapped in a net of intrigues in medieval Venice where it was a doge eat doge existence.

Lady Valerie suddenly cried, "Good heavens! Unless my eyes deceive me . . . in there . . . at the corner of the bar . . . the Scotland Yard man—whatsisname, you know—questions about Lisa and all that nonsense . . . "

Sylvia felt faint.

The Pakistani jostled Dylan who returned the discourtesy with a vulgar epithet. Suddenly fists flew and women screamed and Madame Vilna rummaged in her purse. Joe Gordon struggled to separate Dylan and his adversary. Lady Valerie yelled, "It *is* him . . . Roberts . . . with the priest."

Dylan Wake screamed "I've been stabbed! I've been stabbed!"

Madame Vilna grabbed Lady Valerie's arm, "Our Dylan has been stabbed!"

Lady Valerie pivoted and saw Dylan clutching his left arm, shrieked, stared at a small patch of filthy floor, and decided against fainting.

Edna pushed her way indoors to the bar and spoke hastily to the astonished Channing Roberts and Max Van Larsen.

Joe Gordon caught Dylan Wake as he began to sink to the floor.

The young Pakistani struggling in the powerful grips of two gentleman yelled his innocence.

Madame Vilna had a protective arm around Sylvia who was watching Edna's progress. Having caught one loving glimpse of the disguised Max, a much relieved Sylvia watched him and Channing Roberts hastily heading towards the exit.

"Get a doctor!" Joe Gordon shouted.

"*Gendarmes!*" That was Vilna.

Edna with an effort attempted to rejoin her group.

"Urmph!"

"Urmph!"

"Uuuurmmmpppphhhhh!"

Edna was back.

Dylan Wake was stretched out on the floor, a trickle of blood oozing from his left arm. Lady Valerie had borrowed Gordon's handkershief and was applying a tourniquet. Behind them, Harry Sanders had suddenly appeared. Dylan opened his eyes and the first person he saw was the chauffeur.

Harry Sanders bent over and inquired, "How are you, me old darlin'?"

Half an hour later, two ambulance attendants were lifting Dylan Wake from the back of an ambulance. The Rolls Royce pulled up and Lady Valerie was the first to emerge.

"Dylan! Dylan! Speak to me, Dylan!"

The others were out of the car and followed Lady Valerie and the stretcher into the hospital. Harry Sanders remained behind the wheel merrily whistling "The Kerry Dancers."

While the others were giving assistance to the admittance clerk, Edna was startled to see Evelyn Blair emerge fom an elevator dabbing at her eyes with a handkerchief.

"Well, for goodness' sake! Isn't that that reporter thing from the airport, Sylvia?"

Sylvia looked up sharply. "Why heavens! It's Miss Blair, isn't it?"

Evelyn Blair was staring down at Dylan Wake whose eyes had just fluttered open.

"Whatever it is," Evelyn Blair said venomously, "I hope it's fatal." She turned to Lady Valerie and Madame Vilna. "Nelly Locke is dead."

CHAPTER
nine

"*My* Nelly?" said Madame Vilna incredulously. She teetered. Joe Gordon leapt to her side and steadied her.

"My *understudy*?" whispered Lady Valerie as she retrieved the sachet from her purse and waved it frantically under her nose like a semaphore.

"My God," they heard Dylan Wake croaking.

"They say she gassed herself," said Evelyn Blair in a choked voice, "but I think different!"

The admittance clerk signalled the attendants and they began wheeling Dylan down the corridor. Lady Valerie made a move to follow, but Evelyn Blair stepped in her path.

"I say Nelly Locke was murdered!"

"Don't tell me," grated Lady Valerie, "tell the police."

"Is there an all-night synagogue nearby?" Madame Vilha inquired of the admittance clerk. The clerk, a young Arab, recoiled.

The elevator doors opened again and disgorged two police officers. One approached Evelyn Blair and said, "Would you accompany us please, miss? We'd like to take your statement."

Madame Vilna pressed forward and clutched the young officer's arm. His name was Owen Willoughby and in years to come he would always remember the

Vilna grip with pain and admiration. "I was well acquainted with the deceased. What happened?"

Willoughby gurgled, "Gas . . . suicide."

"And that is *all*?" Vilna and Willoughby were almost nose to nose.

"That is all I can tell you at the moment, Madame. *Please* . . . my *arm*."

Vilna released him and sought Sylvia's eye and found it. She swiftly gestured her to one side and Sylvia dutifully followed. The others watched Evelyn Blair depart with the two police officers. Edna was telling the admittance clerk, "From past experience let me tell you, that's only a superficial knife wound. It was no gusher, if you know what I mean."

Lady Valerie and Joseph Gordon shared a bench further down the hall deep in a private conversation.

In a nearby stairwell, Madame Vilna and Sylvia were sequestered. At the moment, Sylvia was staring aghast at the older woman.

"You didn't!"

"But I did!" exclaimed Vilna. Her purse was open and she was holding cuticle scissors in her left hand. "I punctured him with this!"

"But Vilna! That's *assault*!"

"Nonsense, it was a ploy. I created a diversion away from Max, did I not?"

"But that poor little Pakistani . . ."

"In due time I shall explain all to the charming Mr. Roberts. He will of course applaud my quick thinking. It is fortunate I was able to recall on the spur of the tedious moment my triumph in *Shribe Mir Nisht Mehr Keiner Vechter*, which is perhaps more familiar to you as W. Somerset Maugham's *The Letter*. And me old darlin' will most certainly understand and forgive me as he enjoys wallowing in a dramatic situation like a bored sow in a mud puddle. But I merely thought you should know as my conscience gnaws at me like a Jewish mother pleading with a son to study to be a dentist.

"Now then, I think it is of the utmost importance that at the present we disassociate ourselves from Gordon and Lady Valerie, return to your hotel, and communicate with Scotland Yard. Room service can alleviate our hunger, and mine at the moment is uncommonly voracious. There was something I overheard at the races which I must impart immediately to appropriate ears."

"What? Tell me!"

Vilna patted Sylvia's cheek with affection. "A twice-told tale frequently loses its effect. I reserve comment until we are joined by Mr. Roberts and Max." She was rubbing her chin with her knuckles. "Leonard Greystoke's death I'm not so sure about, but add to it Nelly Locke—poor little misbegotten ingénue, as what ingénue isn't—that already is not so *ay ay ay*. And the reporter woman is obviously not one given to idle accusations."

"She most certainly isn't."

Vilna gestured with her head. "Come, darling Sylvia. *Suivez-moi!*" Sylvia followed her.

"It's a mere scratch!" announced Edna smugly as Vilna and Sylvia rejoined her and the others. "He'll be down as soon as they apply the band-aid."

Lady Valerie was holding tightly to Joseph Gordon's arm. "I'm afraid you'll have to forgive me, but I'm not feeling up to the rest of the evening."

Sylvia chimed in with alacrity. "Oh, I'm so glad somebody said something. I know exactly how you feel. Joe, will you forgive us?"

"Of course, Sylvia," said Joe with understanding. "I'll have Harry drive you girls home. I'll wait for Dylan." He rubbed Valerie's hand. "Are you sure you'll be all right?"

Edna and Sylvia exchanged glances.

Valerie nodded her head as she smiled weakly. "Quite all right, my dear. But Leonard and Nelly and that fiend attacking Dylan . . . "

Vilna coughed politely and took a tighter grip on her purse.

Lady Valerie's hand flew to her head. "It's a cornucopeia of tragedy!"

Sylvia poked Edna whose eyes had crossed.

Said Joe, "I'll give Harry his instructions," and left.

The elevator doors parted and Dylan emerged. His left arm was in a sling and his jacket hung over his shoulders. His hair was uncombed over a haggard face. Madame Vilna rushed to him with arms prepared for an embrace.

"My Hamlet! My star! Who pierced you, has pierced my heart!"

"Ah, me old darlin'. I was born under an unlucky star! The little folk must have turned their backs when I emerged from me sainted mother's womb."

Sylvia and Edna clucked around him like he was head rooster in the barnyard and Dylan was led outside to the waiting car, avoiding Lady Valerie's searching eyes. Upon seeing Harry Sanders, his feet froze. Harry smiled.

"A bit weak in the pins, old boy?" inquired Gordon.

Dylan's feet came to life again and he entered the back seat followed by the four women and Joseph Gordon. The drive to the Dorchester took them past the American Embassy in Grosvenor Square, where police were trying to quell a mob of women hurling rocks at the imposing edifice.

"What in heaven's name is *that*!" cried Sylvia.

Said Gordon matter-of-factly, "Another demonstration by Wives for Peace."

At his office in Scotland Yard, Channing Roberts' eyes darted from Max Van Larsen to Owen Willoughby, the officer in the Nelly Locke case.

"They're going to perform an autopsy," Willoughby said, "but the examining medico is pretty positive the thump on the head did her in. Skull was bashed at the base and that's usually fatal."

Max folded his arms and addressed Roberts. "You may have to declare the Old Avon a disaster area." A few seconds earlier, they had been informed of the attack on Dylan Wake.

Roberts toyed with a letter-opener. "If the autopsy proves positive, Max, I can't delay an investigation until after the weekend. There'll be pressure."

"What odds will you take that everyone has an iron-clad alibi?"

"Thank you, old chap, but I've done all my gambling for the week." He stared at two yellow tickets on his desk. "I suppose I'll never collect my winnings on Witches' Brew. What a beautiful long shot."

The phone rang and he answered it. His face brightened. "Hello my dear. Quite a bit of excitement your first day here."

Max sat up.

"What?" inquired Roberts of Sylvia. "Yes, that's quite possible. He's with me. Yes indeed. As soon as possible." He hung up and addressed Max. "In the mood for a quiet supper at the Dorchester?"

When the Rolls Royce pulled away from the Dorchester, Lady Valerie pressed the button for the automatic window that isolated them from Harry Sanders. She positioned herself facing Dylan Wake.

"What have you done?"

Dylan was staring out the window with half-shut eyes. "What the hell are you talking about?"

"Nelly Locke!"

Joe Gordon was sitting forward with fingers interlaced between his legs. He was finding Dylan's voice strangely colorless.

"I'm as shocked as you are." Dylan might have been repeating the audition he gave as a neophyte twelve years earlier.

"You said she dropped in on you this evening!"

Dylan came to life as he turned to her and shouted, "And then dropped right out. She was meeting Evelyn Blair at *her* flat, not *mine*." He sank back against the pluch seat. "Poor Little Nelly. How sad. Cut down in her prime."

"What did she want?" persisted Valerie.

"When?"

"When she came to see you, damn you!"

"She wanted me to marry her."

Lady Valerie smirked and told Joe Gordon, "Little Nell was in the throes of another pregnancy."

"The poor kid," said Joe and it was his turn to stare out the window.

"She wasn't much of an actress," said Lady Valerie examining a fingernail. Dylan's eyes were cobra-lidded again.

"Gas," he muttered, "that's not Nelly at all."

"Evelyn Blair apparently agrees with you," said Gordon. "And she's no fool." He abandoned the window for Lady Valerie. "It'll mean the police again."

Lady Valerie stifled a yawn. "It's the police anyway, thanks to Dylan's minor scratch."

"Piss on you!" hissed Dylan, then shook his head in frustration. "That bloody wog! Of all the bloody wogs in London, *he* had to be at White City. Damn! I never collected my win."

"None of us collected," said Joseph Gordon.

"My darlings," said Lady Valerie, her voice curdled cream, "fasten your seatbelts for a bumpy weekend. Unless my eyes deceived me, and they rarely do, I saw more then I was intended to see at the track tonight."

In Judith Sondergaard's ground floor bedroom at the rear of Astoroth House, Vernon Mayhew held the housekeeper in a tight embrace.

"My Adonis," she whispered in his ear.

"Yes, my Sappho," he whispered back.

"Don't look now but I think someone's watching at the window."

"You jest."

"I'm rarely given to levity in moments of passion. There's a voyeur at the window."

Gently they drew apart as she held his face in her hands.

"You get into bed," she instructed him with dulcet tones "while I repair to the kitchen and phone the boys at their zoo quarters. Be nonchalant."

He pulled her to him, snuggled her neck, and then released her. Delicately, like a puff ball caught in a late summer breeze, she wafted to the door, opened it, turned, blew him a kiss, and left. Sir Vernon pulled back the bedcovers and smiled to himself, then facing the window, unzipped his fly.

Outside the window, the nubile Esmeralda's face flushed with erotic excitement. Oh my God, she thought to herself with an unbridled inner passion, oh my God, I *am* a true Shmeckelecker (which was the family name). I am my father's true daughter and his father's true granddaughter, for are they not both Vesuvian hot bloods?

Inside the bedroom, Sir Vernon was removing his trousers with the professional éclat of a celebrated ecdysiast. Humming "The Stripper" under his breath, he was grateful for the ballet lessons he'd been forced to endure as a child. Judith Sondergaard re-entered the room as he began unbuttoning the shirt with his left hand, his right hand holding a bed post as his hips wriggled in a non-too-subdued shimmy.

Judith laughed what she considered her tinkling laugh (which was actually the simulated soundtrack of two courting alley cats crashing into a row of garbage cans). "Let me . . . oh darling, let *me*," she pleaded sultrily as she sinuously stalked over to him and commandeered the unbuttoning.

Outside, a blend of perspiration and hair grease trickled down the panting Esmeralda's face. In the near-stupor of her ersatz thrall, she did not hear the two men stealthily coming up behind her.

From outside, Judith and Vernon heard one of the zoo attendant's shout, "Got her!" But they couldn't have cared less.

In the suite at the Dorchester, Sylvia Plotkin's lips were hotly pressed against Max Van Larsen's like a mustard plaster. When they finally drew apart, she stroked his stubbly chin and whispered, "You look so tired, Max."

Max put his arm around her waist and they joined Madame Vilna, Edna, and Channing Roberts at a buffet table that had been set up prior to their arrival. Madame Vilna was discoursing on the evening's adventures, punctuating her remarks with a turkey drumstick, and was probably the only conductor in living or past history who in a course of a recital succeeded in demolishing the baton. In a brief and breathless recap, she succeeded in stringing together an informative necklace from which dangled "Dylan Wake stabbed by me as a diversion and I found it very diverting," Evelyn Blair's insistence that Nelly Locke had been murdered, the weekend invitation to Astoroth House, and then, finally, what she had overheard at the dog track.

"What the Pakistani said to Dylan prior to the fracas was *most* interesting. Among other things he called him a 'ponse', which in English argot is more familiarly known as a kept man, insinuated Dylan had been instrumental in possibly betraying the Pakistani's brother who attempted to enter this country illegally, and may have trafficked in drugs." She paused for both effect and to spear a slice of cold ham, and then added, "And then the Pakistani mentioned something vile about Astoroth House which I didn't quite catch, as by then fists were flying and Lady Valerie was nosing you both out like a pig digging truffles. Most valuable, is this not?"

Madame Vilna's compendium pleased Roberts and Max no end and they both expressed their gratitude.

"I am a mistress at the art of eavesdropping," admitted Vilna with unabashed pride, "an art developed during a long South American tour in *Ah Voo Shpilst Du Mitt Der Chotchkerlach*, which is perhaps more cognizant to you as *Toys In The Attic*."

"I'm frightened."

All eyes were on Edna.

"Well, I *am*. We came here to help find a missing girl and the source of Max's unfortunate indisposition—but *murder*! Do you realize any one of us could be a target? And what about poor Gypsy Marie and Quasi? Out there alone and unprotected at the enchanted cottage."

"Trust Gypsy," said Max knowledgeably, "you can bet your bottom shilling she's industriously ploughing ahead with her setting-up exorcises.

"I assure you, Miss Shelley," Roberts suavely interjected, "Scotland Yard is taking every precaution."

"Really, Edna," said Sylvia with a rare hauteur, "you're too old to turn chicken!"

"I'm not in the least bit frightened for myself," replied the editor with nostrils flaring, "I just want to be sure everybody's aware we're not out to swat flies at a Sunday school picnic."

129

Said Vilna nonchalantly, "Eat something, Edna dear. Look how you look." Her body shook with laughter and her caparisons jingled merrily. "I myself am most sanguine about the coming weekend. Does not the hunter sportingly alert the fox with his 'tantivy, tantivy, yoicks.' Well, my dear, likewise are we yoicking away. Conglomerately, *they* are worried, and when people worry, they grow frantic and careless and make fatal errors. Undoubtedly a fatal error has already been committed with the murder of the luckless Locke."

"Leonard Greystoke was also murdered." Max thought Vilna was about to faint. Her hand (holding a fork with potato salad of sand dune proportion) was frozen at her mouth. She boomed:

"But *why? Why?* Given a bit more time, he would have expired from natural causes!" She leaned forward eagerly. "How was it done?" Roberts explained and Vilna shook her head sadly. "Undoubtedly administered by whomever held the paper cup to his lips."

Roberts pounced and Vilna spent the next five minutes trying to recreate the scene of Greystoke's presumed heart attack. Who among his so-called ministering angels might have been responsible for placing the celestial halo around his head. Dylan Wake, Lady Valerie, Nelly Locke, and various other members of the company has been in a position to administer the hemlock.

Sylvia Plotkin, as a recent initiate into the new American crime writer's association, the Clue-Clucks Clan, silently attempted to mine additional nuggets from earlier conversations with Lady Valerie and Dylan, and her train of thought eventually pulled into a depot. She tugged at Max's sleeve and he followed her to the other side of the room.

"Is Joe Gordon wealthy?"

Max weighed his words carefully before dispensing them. "He earns a good income."

"Good enough to race dogs, bet heavily, and live high on the hog with a rented Rolls Royce and chauffeur?"

Max shoved his hands in his trouser pockets and rocked gently on his heels. "I know what you're getting at. But Lisa's his *daughter*. He dotes on her."

"You're so sure? And what *about* that chauffeur, that Harry Sanders. Not only an ex-con, but a stomper yet." She repeated rapidly hers and Edna's repartee with Sanders on the drive from the airport.

"He was in love with Lisa," Max informed her.

"Oh?" She turned it over in her mind a moment. "Does Joe know?"

"I don't think so. At least he never mentioned it to me."

Sylvia's next question sprang from her mouth like a greyhound from its trap. "Was Dylan having an affair with Lisa by any chance."

"By every chance."

"And Nelly no like."

"No like at all."

"Do you remember a reporter named Nick Hasting?"

"No like at all. A very close chum of Valerie's."

"Aha. Max . . . you and Roberts have a theory, don't you? I mean a very logical theory as to what's behind the hanky-panky at Astoroth House, don't you?"

"We'd be damned fools if we didn't."

"So?" she intoned coquettishly, "share a morsel with a starving friend."

Max kissed her forehead and then took her hands and held them lovingly in his own. "I love you but you're a blabbermouth."

Sylvia jerked her hands away. "But you send your blabbermouth to tread where angels fear!"

The phone rang and Sylvia angrily reached out and answered it. "It's for you, Mr. Roberts," said Sylvia in a voice stiff with starch. When Roberts took the phone, she strode back to Edna and Madame Vilna who were lifting demitasse cups to their lips and munching petit fours.

Roberts hung up the phone and announced, "That was the result of Miss Locke's autopsy. It was murder."

Sylvia was still bristing. She whispered a question in Vilna's ear and Vilna studied Sylvia gravely. Sylvia snapped her fingers impatiently and Vilna dug in her purse, brought out an address book, riffled the pages, and pointed to the information Sylvia sought. Committing what she had read to memory, Sylvia loped across the room to the bedroom, entered, and slammed the door shut.

Edna jumped and asked Max, "What the hell's eating her?"

"Teacher's mad," said Max as he poured himself some coffee, "I didn't give her the right answers."

Dylan Wake was stretched out on his couch holding the phone to his ear. He had rapidly recovered from the initial surprise when Sylvia identified herself.

"I'd be delighted to have lunch tomorrow," he purred into the mouthpiece," Vilna usually calls a break around one." He suggested a popular pub in the vicinity of the Old Avon, and then hung up. He lay back and stared at the specked ceiling while gently stroking the area where he had been punctured.

Greystoke was poisoned. Nelly was killed by a bash on the skull. It's important Sylvia sees me alone.

And Vilna heard everything the filthy wog had said at the dogs.

He suffered a sudden, violent fit of coughing, meanwhile cautioning himself, "Courage, Camille." The coughing subsided and he sat up with his feet touching the floor, the right foot tapping lightly. He whispered aloud:

" 'Here hung those lips that I have kissed I know not how oft.' "

Nelly's lips. Lisa's. Valerie's. So many lips.

" 'Where be your gibes now?' "

And all had gibed. Is the joke still on me, he wondered. Has it been arranged for me to take the rap? What's Plotkin up to. How much do *they* really know?

How much do I really know?

And who *did* stab me? It wasn't the wog, he wasn't holding any weapon.

Sanders was grinning down at me. *How are you, me old darlin'.*

Dylan's head almost ached at the memory of Sanders' feet attacking his skull like an Italian vintner running amuck in a tub of grapes.

He'll do me yet, he thought grimly. He's waiting. He's biding his time. Cons know how to wait.

If he doesn't, somebody else will.

He wailed aloud.

"Oh Jesus! Give me an extension, Jesus baby! I know I'm living on borrowed time! But let me open in *Hamlet*! Give me this one opportunity to show the frigging world what I can really do! Oh Jesus, have a heart. Keep in mind, me old darlin', You had a second chance!"

Dame Augusta Mayhew was bristling into the telephone like a Pekinese deprived the harbor of its favorite lap. "Really, Valerie," she yapped, "we agreed Nelly had to go, but not *this* way." She sat up sharply. "What? *What*? Leonard *too*? Yes, yes,, I know Nick has ways of finding these things out . . . but *Leonard*! It's too ridiculous! Why he wouldn't harm a fly unless it was unzipped. This is bad business indeed. Extremely bad business. Himself will be most displeased. *Most* displeased. No, no, no. Let him read it for himself in the newspapers. I'm going back to my film on the telly. What? Some old American thriller as usual. On BBC 2, darling. It's that enchanting girl who played Al Jolson's wife. Who? That's right, Evelyn Keyes. Well," she snuggled closer to the phone, "she's this typhoid carrier see, and she's on the loose in New York infecting everyone.

133

Yes," she laughed lightly, "she is an infectious actress. Anyway, she's involved with that actor with the cleft in his chin. Not Cary Grant, dear, this one has an accent. Charles Korvette or something like that. Korvin? He should have changed it. Well anyway, there's Evelyn in Grand Central Station right *now* . . . "

At midnight precisely, Gypsy Marie Rachmaninoff's wagon was hidden in a grove of trees adjacent to a lonely country crossroads. The horses were blessedly docile, thanks to the feed bags hung around their necks. Only an inquisitive owl saucily inquired, "Whoo? Whoo?"

"With any luck," whispered Gypsy Marie, "I'll tell you Sunday."

She crept cautiously to the end of the road. The only light was the beam of a yellow moon that hung transfixed in the sky like an overfried egg yolk. Then in the distance, she heard the soft purr of a motor, in a few moments, a black Volkswagon pulled up and blinked its headlights three times. Marie stepped into the roadway and caused her corncob pipe to glow three times. The front left door of the Volkswagon sprung open and from it leapt the disguised Quasimodo. Gypsy Marie stepped forward into the moonlight and hugged her priceless changeling to her lavender-scent bosom. The Volkswagon pulled away and disappeared as Marie rapidly gave Quasimodo further instruction, indoctrinated him into the denizens of Rom Magyar's troupe, and then complimented him on the effectiveness of his female disguise.

"Oh boy, oh boy," muttered the disgruntled hunchback, "if they ever find out about this back on Eighth Street, I'll have a new popularity I won't know how to cope with."

Gypsy Marie lifted him into the wagon, removed the feed bags from the horses, clambered onto the front seat of the wagon, grasped the reins and the whip, and directed the overfed nags back to the camp.

She told Quasimodo-Salmonella all he needed to know about Astoroth House, its occupants, and primarily, the one whose friendship he was to pursue, Lord Carson.

"But remember," she cautioned, "there is great danger there. And that housekeeper is wise beyond her years." Gypsy Marie cackled a Romany cackle. "But I think I've got her where I want her. Tomorrow . . . early . . . we'll drop in on her."

A cloud suddenly covered the moon and Gypsy Marie looked at the sky with apprehension.

"Holy Romany! That's a dark omen. When the clouds cover a full moon on a Thursday midnight, you can bet your clouded crystal ball there'll be dark doings in the countryside."

Quasimodo shivered and nestled against his mother. Gypsy Marie stared down at her pride and joy contentedly.

"I'm a very lucky mother," she whispered to her child, "your father would be proud of you, if I could remember his name."

Shortly after midnight at the Dorchester suite, Max and Detective Inspector Roberts offered to see Madame Vilna home, cautioning her they would have to leave the hotel by the service door. "Once," intoned Vilna ripely, "I was smuggled from a gentleman's home in a laundry basket. Oooh! Wah, hah, hah, hah, hah!" Her laughter shook the room like a passing truck. "I am a mistress at disguises. Oh how I fooled the audiences in *Ich'll Dir Zuggen Alles Oz Du Fregst Mir*, which is perhaps more familiar to you as *Witness For The Prosecution*. Goodnight, Sylvia. Goodnight Edna." She kissed Sylvia warmly and pecked lightly at Edna's cheek.

Max put his hands on Sylvia's stiff shoulders. "You're a pain in the ass but I love you."

Sylvia melted and kissed him but did not tell him of her next day's rendezvous with Dylan Wake.

Edna crossed to the door, opened it, and stifled a scream.

"What the hell is *that*?" she cried.

Tacked to the door with a thin string around its broken neck was the stiff corpse of a bird.

"That," said Max, "is either a warped joke or a warning. It's to let you know there's danger ahead. It was undoubtedly put there by a witch."

CHAPTER
ten

As Gypsy Marie braked the wagon near her tent at the edge of the camp, she heard an infernal uproar. Followed by Quasimodo-Salmonella, she nimbly alighted and ran toward the main campfire, where an enraged Rom Magyar surrounded by his wailing followers, was hurling epithets and shaking his fists at the sky.

"It is the curse of the Shmeckeleckers! "He saw Gypsy Marie and ran to meet her. "It is Esmeralda!"

"She's pregnant?"

"Worse! She's missing! I looked in her tent and her bed of roses has not been slept in! I tell you it's a wicked switch! Somebody's stolen a gypsy!"

"Calm yourself, calm yourself. When did you last see her?"

Rom Magyar sank to his knees. "Shortly after ten. She said she was going to sleep as she wanted an early start in the morning to pick juniper beries for her father's home distilled gin." He looked up into Gypsy Marie's motherly face. "She's a good child underneath all that filth. Do you suppose . . . ?" He was back on his feet again. "Do you suppose she has gone *there*?"

"Where?" asked Gypsy Marie innocently as though she hadn't already guessed.

"To that infernal house of the devil! To join in their unnatural orgies."

"Really, Magyar, that's weekends only. Come with me to my tent. I would a word with you."

"What are words when at this very moment they may be defiling my semi-precious jewel!"

Gypsy Marie grabbed his hand. "Permit a cooler head to prevail, Magyar. It is not too late for a Shmeckelecker to learn a thing or two."

His head shot forward and Gypsy Marie shuddered from the wave of rancid breath. "What is it you know, woman?"

Gypsy Marie winked, gestured with her head, took Quasimodo's hand, and led the way to her tent. Magyar pointed at the hunchbacked figure.

"And what is *that*?"

"My daughter, Salmonella. She's just returned from finishing school. Say hello to Magyar, Salmonella my beloved."

Quasimodo turned, gulped, and courtsied. Magyar smiled and patted the hump. "It is good to meet a short, well-brought-up daughter. Do you like camping, Salmonella?"

"What did you have in mind?"

Marie grabbed the boy's hand and pulled him into the tent followed by the disconsolate Magyar. Marie then put her hands on her hips and fixed Magyar with a fierce eye. "I swear you to secrecy by the Transylvanian Code of your ancestor, Melchior the Multiplier, that what I am about to tell you, you will not even repeat to yourself. Do you so swear?"

"I so swear."

"Good. Now what I am about to tell you will cause you

greater concern for Esmeralda's well-being." Magyar gasped. "But you will then understand why I must plead your forbearance in abstaining from besieging the wicked Astoroth House. Would you like a beer?"

What's a nice girl like me doing shackled to the wall of a subterranean chamber, wondered the usually non-too-bright Esmeralda. Her windowless cell held a cot, a wash basin, a chamber pot, and an oil lamp, suspended from a nail and flickering dimly. She had recognized her two captors, the zoo attendants, Hank and Mervyn, and could still feel the pressure of Hank's sweaty hand over her mouth, his other locking her hands together behind her back, while Mervyn held her feet.

Well, she mused morosely, I wanted adventure and I got it, but this is more then I reckoned on. Dads will have a conniption and once he rescues me will surely apply the birch to my back. How often has he warned me what could I expect with no mother to guide me. Mother? Mother, are you happy in that cave in Granada with that young rascal who swore he was a Bourbon and showed you the bottle to prove it?

"Help!" she said meekly, the ample chain making it possible for her to recline on the cot.

What will they do to me, she wondered. Torture? with an inward groan; starvation? with a sign of despair; Rape? with a lascivious smile.

She cocked her ears.

What's *that* I hear? That noise like shuffling feet, those curses and execrations. There are people going by the door!

"Help!" she shouted, "Help!"

Mervyn's face appeared in the small aperture cut into the thick wooden door of her cell.

"Shut your face, you snooping gypsy whore!" he growled.

"I'm not a snoop," said Esmeralda with a pout. "And you better let me out of here or there'll be a curse on your head!"

Mervyn cackled villainously and disappeared.

This is a charnal house, Esmeralda now realized with panic. Dads warned me this is the Devil's own home! *The Devil.*

The frightened girl lowered her head and sobbed bitterly.

"Murder, drugs, illegal immigration, white slavery, and what the hell do we get but a stinking dead canary tacked to the door," complained Edna as she climbed into bed.

Sylvia, seated at the dressing table with cold cream lavishly smeared on her face, gave in to an urge and printed MAX on her cheek with her index finger.

"I'm lunching with Joe Gordon tomorrow," Edna told her.

Sylvia turned her head. "When did that happen?"

"At the dogs, before the fuss. And don't *you* try to horn in."

"Thank you very much beloved friend, but I've made my own arrangements."

Edna plumped up her pillows and sat back with her knees drawn up. "Such as?"

"Dylan Wake."

"He's very cute."

Said Sylvia flatly, "He's no Max Van Larsen. This is strictly business, though he doesn't know it yet."

"You be careful."

"Likewise."

"Let's meet back here at three to compare notes."

"We'll meet back here at three to *pack* for the weekend." Sylvia could have sworn she heard Edna whimper, which was a sound normally quite alien to Edna. "You *are* frightened."

"Out of my skull. Supposing Saturday night they ask us to do a trick or an incantation or conjure up an *obeah* or whatever the hell us witches are supposed to come up with at the dark of the moon. What *then?*"

"Leave it to me," said Sylvia with confidence, "I've been rehearsing." She cackled ominously at her own reflection. "They'll soon learn there's no witch like a Zionist witch!"

Gypsy Marie Rachmaninoff held a homing pigeon in her hands and stroked its back gently as she cooed into its ear. "Scotland Yard . . . south by southeast and don't stop to get naughty over Windsor Castle. If the wind blows you off your course, just look for a long blue tape below, that'll be the Thames." She waved her hand over the pigeon's head. "May no chicken hawks cross your path."

She released the pigeon. Swiftly it soared overhead, dipped its wings in a sentimental gesture of farewell, and then shot forward like a zephyr. Gypsy Marie tiptoed back into the tent and placed another hand-embroidered blanket over the sleeping Quasimodo. She thought to herself, which is the more endearing, mother love or flying pigeons? Anyway, Roberts will soon know of the misfortune that has befallen the unfortunate slut Esmeralda. He'll have to understand why I had to take Magyar into my confidence. Besieging Astoroth House now could blow the whole caper. Ah, the Shmeckeleckers are truly an accursed lot!

At three A.M., Max Van Larsen sat in a chair by the window of his lonely bed-sitter, staring out the window in another attempt to jog his memory into unlocking the secret of his near-fatal weekend at Astoroth House.

"I know I discovered something that previous night, I *know* I did. I remember the highjinks at midnight— more like a bad tableau at Radio City Music Hall—but then I snuck away on my own. I went into the house to look for something. I knew I wouldn't be missed because the orgy was in full swing, Lady Valerie dancing naked in the maze and Dame Augusta and that cherubic little vicar doing the Charleston. As to what the others were doing, Max shuddered at the recall. Nick Hastings swinging naked by his knees from a tree branch, the vicar's housekeeper misbehaving outrageously with a chattering chimpanzee, that sextette of girls interweaving with each other in some sort of trance . . .

Max snapped his fingers and bolted out of the chair.

Some short of trance!

The door to the hidden memory had unlocked. He remembered. He remembered it all.

His finger itched to dial Channing Roberts at home but a glance at his wristwatch told him at this hour it would be too thoughtless. It could wait until morning. Now things needed to be tied together. What were the links between Astoroth House and the two murders?

Who was the master mind?

Who was running the operation?

Lady Valerie? Dame Augusta? Sir Vernon? Sondergaard? Maybe Nick Hastings? *Dylan Wake*? Who? Who? Who?

It couldn't be the butler because Astoroth House didn't have a butler. Max lit a cigarette and pondered further. It had to be someone with connections abroad, someone with the sort of rare, inventive mind capable of perfecting so bizarre an outrage. Max crossed to his suitcase, found a pad of paper, returned to the chair by the window, and began makin notes. The first name he very carefully wrote was JOE GORDON.

The following morning, Evelyn Blair's impassioned article in the *Morning Herald* came like a bombshell to her Fleet Street competitors and rocked her faithful following. It had been written with the bravura of a doped-up rock star playing an electric guitar while standing in a pool of water. It was as pointed as an invitation from a prostitute standing in a Shepherd's Market doorway. It was underlined with the ironic bitterness of a divorce case. Stopping within a hairline of slander and libel, the article—without actually naming names—cleverly linked Astoroth House to the murders of Nelly Locke and Leonard Greystoke. That news had been released to Fleet Street in time for the morning editions, and Evelyn's editor very carefully placed the information in the column adjoining Evelyn's.

Re-reading her own article over morning coffee, Evelyn Blair felt the exhilaration of a detonation expert who had set off an intricate charge of dynamite. This article, she decided, will either get me a Global News Award or murdered. She lowered the paper and stared at one of two photographs on her desk.

"Dear Lisa," she whispered, "dear, dear Lisa."

Evelyn's readership was legion due to the large circulation of her newspaper.

In his study, seated at his desk behind which hung the multi-pinned map, Oscar Treble clucked his tongue, shook his head, and added another teaspoon of sugar to his tea. Amanda Brush, his housekeeper, was attacking a sideboard with a feather duster and wondering aloud about the pedigree of the priest who was now a definite addition to the weekend. Detective-Inspector Roberts had phoned Mr. Treble earlier and completed the arrangements. Mr. Treble was re-reading Evelyn Blair's article.

"Oh dear, oh dear, oh dear," Miss Brush heard the vicar murmuring, "oh dear, oh dear, oh dear."

Miss Brush indicated his tea, "Too cold?"

"Oh no, my dear," said the troubled vicar, "too hot."

Lady Valerie's cab driver had been instructed to pick

up Dame Augusta, and when she entered the taxi she brandished her rolled up newspaper in Valerie's face.

"You've read the Blair woman this morning?"

"I always read Blair, you know that."

"I phoned himself."

"And?"

"He's thinking."

"What about the weekend?"

"As scheduled. It would look much too suspicious to cancel in the light of this morning's event."

"Something tells me we'd better prepare our travelling bags and peasant disguises."

"Let us not panic, my dear Valerie. Our mastermind is a master mind. He'll think of something."

"If Plan X is put into operation, what do we do with my son? What do we do with Carson?"

"I'm afraid my dear, that is between your conscience and Satan."

Joseph Gordon read Evelyn Blair's article in the back seat of the Rolls Royce headed towards a session at the House of Parliament. He heard Big Ben tolling and it was like a series of sledgehammer blows on his skull. Bloody Blair bitch, he thought to himself, I told her to *wait*. I said *wait* Eveyln, give it time, give it until *Monday* . . . but a woman scorned is indeed a vessel of wrath.

"You read Blair this morning?" he inquired of Harry Sanders as they were driving past Westminister Abbey.

"Yes, Mr. Gordon."

"She shouldn't have done it. Not yet. She should have waited."

"Not many people know how to wait, Mr. Gordon. Us cons, we know how to wait. But that's one hell of an article."

Hell, thought Joseph Gordon, is absolutely on the nose.

Judith Sondergaard had read the article aloud that morning to Sir Vernon Mayhew and a piece of toast lodged in his throat. She slammed him on the back for thirty seconds until he disgorged the bread, then resumed her seat at the kitchen table and turned to the back of the paper.

"What are you reading *now*?" growled Sir Vernon.

"The want ads."

In his office, Detective-Inspector Channing Roberts puffed thoughtfully at his pipe as he re-examined the sighting of his hunting rifle. Max Van Larsen sat across from him reading the final sentence of Evelyn Blair's article.

"When that lady takes aim," said Max, "she certainly scores." Roberts was placing the gun in its case and closed the lid. "Bad for us or good for us, Chan?"

"If Astoroth House cancels the weekend, it's very, very bad. And if Astoroth House doesn't cancel, it's very, very dangerous. You're positive what you've told me you uncovered that weekend is correct right down to the last detail?"

"Absolutely positive."

"Good. Then I shall see to the arrangements."

Max flipped open the pad in which he had been making notes most of the night.

"What have you there?" asked Roberts.

"A complete breakdown of everyone involved," explained Max, "in hopes it might give me a clue to the person behind this entire enterprise."

"And what result?"

Max leaned back in his chair, crossed his legs, and spoke a name. Roberts' hand flew up to catch the pipe that was about to drop from his mouth.

"But *how* did you arrive at *that*?"

Max explained at length. When he finished, Roberts realized with astonishment that his hands were trembling. "What do you think?" asked Max.

"What do I *think*? Old boy, if your supposition is correct, this could be your last weekend on Earth!"

Sylvia and Edna's reactions to Evelyn Blair's articles were as disparate as the ideals of Thomas Paine and John Birch.

"Rotten syntax," snapped Edna.

Sylvia's comments were far more eclectic. She thought Evelyn Blair was forthright, brave, honest, and must be invited to join the Women's Liberation Movement.

"You damn fool," said Edna, "don't you know this sort of thing can send those rats scurrying for cover?"

"Any bets?" challenged Sylvia.

Edna ignored the challenge. "Is there a local Hammacher-Schlemmer?"

"Why, for crying out loud?"

"I want to buy a gun. If Astoroth House is still on, should there be any trouble, I don't want to have to put all my faith in my fingernails."

Sylvia was lavishly spreading marmalade on a brioche. "My faith is in Channing Roberts and Max. Let me tell you this, if I know them, by the time we get to Astoroth Houase, the surrounding vicinity will be a beehive of police. Oh my, how my spine is tingling!" She bit into the repast and munched contentedly for a moment.

Edna, who in the meantime had been re-studying the article, suddenly peered at Sylvia over the top of her reading glasses. "Evelyn Blair once had a thing for Joe Gordon, right?"

Sylvia nodded and continued munching, but it was Edna who smacked her lips with relish. Sylvia looked at her inquisitively. "What's with the smacking of the lips?"

"I've got a crazy hunch, that's all."

Sylvia rested an elbow on the table. "About *what*?"

"I'll tell you after lunch."

"Edna, you're giving me indigestion."

Dylan Wake was alone in the Green Room at the Old Avon with a container of tea and the newspaper, held steadily by his now slingless left arm. He couldn't find a line about his altercation at White City and was depressed. The Blair article made his feelings sink even lower.

"You look the picture of health!" boomed Madame Vilna from the doorway as she entered. "How is your arm, my Hamlet. Thank God, it is not your fencing arm, as this morning you all take epeés in hand for the big sword fight!" There was no response from Dylan. "It is Miss Blair that absorbs you?"

Dylan grunted.

Vilna studied the worried-looking actor.

"It is never too late, my dear," she said softly.

He looked up sharply. "for what?"

"To make amends."

"For what," he said again.

"I am sure you know whereof I insinuate. I do not wish to lose a second Hamlet." she turned and slowly left the room feeling Dylan's intense eyes burning into her back.

Quasimodo—now wearing a gypsy blouse and skirt, a pink bandana around his head, and a pair of his mother's earrings dangling from each lobe— disconsolately shlurped his morning oatmeal. Gypsy Marie was ladling another bowl for a still-distraught Rom Magyar who sat cross-legged by the fire outside the tent with palms propping up his sagging head.

He intoned blackly, "That article you read me has robbed me of my usual porcine appetite."

Rom Magyar during a brief period of his own rebellious youth had spent a semester at the Sorbonne. This explained why occasionally his vocabulary was efficacious.

Marie shoved the bowl under his nose. "Eat. You need your strength for the trying hours that lie before us. This is a breakfast of champions."

Listlessly, Rom Magyar accepted the offering and with a spoon made a whirlpool in the porridge in which he imagined Esmeralda drowning. "Supposing my lapis-lazuli is already dead."

"In that house they do not destroy precious jewels," said Gypsy Marie, "they put them in hock."

"Where have you learned all you told me?"

Gypsy Marie's smile was enigmatic. "I get around." They locked eyes. "Trust me, Magyar. You will yet dance at your daughter's wedding and cradle her first born in your arms."

Probably, Gypsy Marie added to herself, the same day.

After two hours of disinterested sightseeing, Edna and Sylvia went their separate paths. At the pub near the Old Avon, Sylvia was directed to the upstairs dining room where Dylan Wake was awaiting her at a table with a Bloody Mary on the rocks for company. They exchanged cheery greetings. Sylvia ordered a Coke and asked Dylan if he had read Evelyn Blair's article.

"It's a load of bollocks," commented Dylan succinctly and with acid.

"I discussed it with Detective-Inspector Channing Roberts this morning," lied Sylvia gracefully, "and he thinks otherwise."

"I didn't know you knew him."

"What? Oh . . . well he *is* a friend of Max's, you know."

"What are you after, Sylvia?"

"When?"

"Now. Me. What are you trying to find out?"

Sylvia plunged in with a recklessness usually reserved for a YWHA swimming pool. "Who gave Max the mickey at Astoroth House?"

"I don't know."

"What's behind the witchcraft scene there?" Her drink

arrived and the few moments it took before the waiter departed gave Dylan a bit of time to think.

"There's nothing," he said, almost drawling each word.

Sylvia switched to a subtler attack. "Vilna tells me you have an amazing talent." Under the table she crossed two fingers of her left hand. "She thinks you'd be perfect for the lead in my new play." She later swore to Edna she finally understood what a novelist meant when they described someone's ears as "pricking."

"You've written a play?"

"A murder mystery." Sylvia dabbed at a bead of Coke on her lip with her paper napkin. "Leonard Soloway has it under option for Broadway and John Quested owns the film rights. I'm a *very* rich, lonely woman and fair game, if you know what I mean."

Dylan's fingers were massaging the stem of his glass. "What about Max?"

"Oh, well. I may as well tell you the truth. It'll be out in the open sooner or later. The chances are very slim he'll recover from this breakdown. That was a very heavy dose he was given of fly ageric." She watched with silent delight as the muscles tightened around his lips. "Thank God it wasn't something really fatal like *Ecballium elaterium* . . . you know, poisoned cucumber juice. Goodness, I'm starved." She examined the menu the waiter had placed at her left elbow while Dylan Wake studied her.

"What's your play about?"

"What?" She looked up quickly. "My play? About? Oh it's a bit old-fashioned but fun. Actually it's got a bit of everything in it. White slavery, would you believe it? And drug-trafficking—audiences never seem to get enough of *that*—and then to pad out the third act I touch on illegal immigration, of which I don't know too much, but by then audiences aren't paying much attention anyway unless half the cast drops their pants or their bras." She

149

managed a demure smile. "I've patterned my hero after Max, of course, and Vilna says you remind her of Max at times and I think I'm beginning to understand what she means. I can see the traces of stubbornness, reticence, dormant passion, and I'm sure you're a lady-killer."

"I'm not stupid, Sylvia Plotkin," he said while signaling for a second drink, "and I don't frighten easily."

"I'm not here to frighten you," said Sylvia cosily, "I'm here to make friends. There's no reason why I shouldn't tell you what I know, inasmuch as Evelyn Blair's practically blown it all this morning. There's illicit goings-on up at Astoroth House, the authorities are on to it, but they lack proof. I just know Scotland Yard is dying to make a deal if they could find somebody to deal with. You *do* know what's going on, don't you?"

He shifted in his seat and stared into the empty, red-stained glass. "Why did Vilna nick me last night?"

"What?"

His eyes met Sylvia's in a steady gaze. "I said why did Vilna stab me last night?"

"V-V-V . . . "

"Vilna."

"Oh dear," uttered Sylvia weakly, "was it Vilna who did that?"

"You know bloody well she did. I spoke to Valerie this morning. She saw Roberts at White City with a priest. She said as much. And to draw everyone's attention away, me old darlin' nicked me. I was pretty good myself, don't you think? I played it for all it was worth. I went through the hospital nonsense and thoroughly enjoyed myself, but I'm not enjoying this."

"Life is not a bowl of cherries."

"It certainly isn't, old fruit, not my life anyway. But it's the only one I've got and I treasure it."

"Tarnished goods."

"Don't be cheeky."

"Where's Lisa Gordon?"

"I don't know."

"Is Joe Gordon mixed up in this?"

"You must be daft"

"Aha! Then there definitely *is* something to be mixed up in! You know after that article I was positive the weekend at Astoroth House would be cancelled."

"Why should it be?" The waiter had brought the second drink and Dylan had gulped a hearty swig. "They've nothing to hide. Evelyn Blair's a frustrated bint. She's mad because they won't let her join in the fun and games. She's tried to get herself asked up there."

"She should be asked this weekend."

"You're cute." Then he thought for a moment. "You know, I'll suggest that very thing to Valerie and Dame Augusta. It might take the sting out of the old broad's tail."

"I gather Evelyn once had a romance with Joe Gordon."

"So I've been told."

"By Lisa?"

"Yes. They were covering the Far East at the same time but that was a very long time ago. Evelyn left her husband and child for Joe and I gather later regretted it."

"How sad for Evelyn. I suppose that's why she poured out all her love to Lisa."

"I suppose so."

"What happened to Lisa that Friday night?"

"What makes you think I was there?"

"I think you got her the invitation. She must have told you she was doing research for me."

"Lisa's a very strange girl. Did you know she loathed her father?" He was enjoying the effect that statement made on Sylvia.

"It never occured to me. I'm glad you told me. That explains something." She was drying her moist palms on the napkin. "But it doesn't explain enough." She hadn't noticed the waiter was in attendance with pencil and pad poised to take their orders.

Dylan Wake's arms were folded. "You haven't lost your appetite, have, you, me old darlin'?"

"Bacon, eggs, and black coffee," responded Sylvia.

"The same," Dylan told the waiter who then departed. "You know Vilna was there that weekend with Max. Hasn't she told you anything?"

"She didn't have much to tell." She did, but Sylvia was not about to share this with Dylan. "Would you like to be considered for my play?"

"You haven't written any play."

It was like a punch in the stomach, his directness, but Sylvia was blessed with the faculty of rapid recovery. "That's right! You can't blame a girl for trying, can you? Now tell me," her elbows were on the table and her hands were interlaced under her chin palms down, "are you also a practicing warlock?"

"I don't have to practice," said Dylan lighting a cigarette, "I'm perfect. You're a sexy bit, Sylvia. How'd you like to go to bed with me?"

"Please Dylan," cooed Sylvia, "not on an empty stomach."

Shortly before lunch and while Max was still with Detective-Inspector Roberts, Gypsy Marie's homing pigeon made its three-point landing into the waiting cage and the message it carried was brought to Roberts' office. He scanned its contents rapidly and repeated to Max the news of Esmeralda's disappearance and the necessity for Marie to take Magyar into her confidence. Max was abnormally elated.

"It's not all that funny," stated Roberts.

"Oh, but it is. Don't we always pray for an adversary's mistake when trying to break a case. Well, here it is, and delivered by another breed of pigeon. What time's my train?"

152

"Six. Charing Cross Station."

"How are you getting up there?"

"I'm motoring, of course. Sorry, I can't offer you a lift, old chap, but that would look too suspicious, wouldn't it?"

"Sweet of the vicar to be this cooperative."

"He couldn't resist the intrigue. Who knows, you might end up a character in his next thriller."

"Urmph," said Joseph Gordon and wondered if Edna would be offended if he widened the island between his chair and her. They were lunching at the Savoy Hotel and Edna had marvelled at the amount of American tourists surrounding them. It was over coffee that she subtly began the interrogation she'd been rehearsing prior to the luncheon.

"Weren't you and Evelyn Blair once a thing?"

Gordon tugged at his collar. "My God, that's ancient history."

"But you're still friends."

"Why, of course. She's been like a mother to Lisa."

"I guess that explains why she's put the heat on this morning. Haven't *you* been pressuring Scotland Yard?"

"Chan Roberts is an old friend. I don't have to pressure him. He's slow," and then added with what Edna interpreted as a tinge of irony, "but steady."

"You *must* tell me how you do it!"

"Do what?" He dreaded what might next emerge from Edna's mouth. His body beneath his clothes was cloyingly damp.

"Remain on such affable terms with that Astoroth House gang to begin with."

"It's not their fault Lisa chose to run away when she was there. Lisa's a very unusual kid. High-strung, imaginative, self-willed, stubborn—"

"For God's sake, add something nice. You're her

father!"

Joe shrugged. "Ah well. She barely knew me until she was entering her teens. I was away so much, and she was at school in Switzerland. We never really got to know each other."

"My hat's off to you. The way you must have had to scrimp to support her. But now you run dogs, hire a Rolls Royce, employ that charming thug, Harry Sanders, and I'll bet you have a stunning apartment."

Gordon was toying with his demi-tasse cup. "I made some lucky investments some years back that finally paid off." He felt if she drew her chair any closer she'd land in his lap.

"Listen, Joe," said Edna cosily, "I'm really such a *yenta* . . . is it true you and Lady Valerie are thattaway?"

He blushed. "Oh now really, Edna!"

"Oh come on, tell me. She's such a gorgeous woman. She certainly doesn't look her age which must be fifty at least if she has a son Nick Hastings' age."

"Sad case, that. He's backward, you know." Edna nodded and began playing with a button on his jacket sleeve. "Got his skull bashed in quite mysteriously one night out at Punting-on-the-Thames."

"Who did such an awful thing?"

"Don't know, not for sure I don't. I think his father has his suspicions. Well, to be exact, he thinks it was young Dylan."

"Heavens!"

"Happened about two years ago when the witch practices began at the house. They get a little wild, you know."

"So do I," said Edna seductively. "Joe, you're such a good reporter. Surely you, like Evelyn Blair, have an idea as to what's *really* going on behind the scenes up there."

"If anything is," said Gordon blandly, "they've got it beautifully camouflaged. It's really all innocent nonsense. Why even the local vicar joins in occasionally. Have you heard that?"

"I've heard that." Sylvia decided to go for broke. "Mr. Roberts had drinks with us yesterday and he thinks Astoroth House might be a front for white slavery, illegal immigration, and dope smuggling, in no particular order. What do *you* think?"

"Do you suppose that's where Evelyn got her material?" he rejoindered swiftly.

"What with all the hullaballoo she's caused, you don't suppose the ladies'll cancel the weekend, do you?"

"Not this weekend."

The way he said it made the base of Edna's spine tingle. It sounded like an order that no one would dare countermand.

CHAPTER
eleven

Judith Sondergaard glanced at the grandfather's clock in the downstairs hallway of Astoroth House, checked her wristwatch, and was satisfied it was positively five minutes past three. She heard Sir Vernon shouting in the study and rushed in just as he slammed the phone down.

"Obviously, that was himself," she said leaning against the door.

"The gypsy girl," said Sir Vernon, "she was a mistake."

Judith crossed to him twirling her chain of keys like a shot put champion warming up for the throw. "It's too late now. She's undoubtedly heard too much from her cell. What do we do?"

"She'll have to go with the others. I'll tell Mervyn to prepare a syringe and start the process."

"The gypsies must have missed her by now. I'm surprised there's been no hue and cry."

"Perhaps they don't read the papers. Maybe they're unaware of what that filthy Blair woman wrote."

"Oh, Vernon," she rushed into his waiting arms and he screamed in pain as the chain of keys struck his vulnerability. "Oh, Vernon," she repeated when it was apparent his pain was abating, "take me away from all this. That gypsy woman's crystal ball wasn't all that clouded. I dread this weekend."

"I can't leave my son."

"There are institutions . . ."

"Never!"

"But the doctor told you he hasn't much longer to live!"

"Oh dear God . . . dear God . . ." He had moved away from her to a window, "the bible was right."

"Hush!"

"It was right, I say. The sins of the fathers . . . there comes that blasted Gypsy woman again. She's got a hunchbacked girl with her." Judith joined him at the window.

"That must be her daughter, Salmonella. Oh look . . . Lord Carson's run to greet the little girl. Oh, it is sweet, they're running off to romp together."

"Find out what the woman knows about the missing girl. But be subtle."

Judith smiled. "Have you ever found me obvious, darling?" He said nothing. "Obviously not."

For the first time that day, Evelyn Blair smiled. Lady Valerie's dulcet tones on the phone a few minutes earlier had tickled her ear and her ego. An invitation to Astoroth House at last. She opened the bottom desk-drawer in her cubicle at the *Morning Herald*, rummaged beneath the pile of papers the drawer contained, and found what she sought. She opened her large purse and placed a revolver in it. Then she shut the drawer, placed the bag on the desk, and phoned Scotland Yard. In a few moments, she was through to Channing Roberts and repeated Lady Valerie's invitation.

She then made a second phone call and again repeated the news. "It looks like we're coming to the moment of truth, angel. Oh, I'm not in the least bit frightened. You'll be there to look after me, won't you?"

While packing for the weekend, Sylvia and Edna swapped what they had learned at their respective luncheons and were immensely pleased with themselves and each other. Then a more sober Edna said, "You realize, of course, we are now marked women."

"Is your courage flagging? Are you still frightened?" Sylvia had decided to borrow a sharp letter-opener and popped it into her suitcase. "This might come in handy."

"You're expecting mail there?"

"Don't be dense. It's for protection in case we need it. Oh boy, oh boy, oh boy." She was rubbing her hands together like a usurer upping his percentage. "What a book this ought to make!"

On stage at the Old Avon, Madame Vilna stood in the center of a large circle formed by her company.

"Everything was beautiful today, my thespians! From the fencing lessons right through to my promising Hamlet's 'Alexander died, Alexander was buried, Alexander returneth to dust.' Very beautiful, Dylan, very beautiful indeed. I coughed at that moment because I could smell the dust, which is by me a compliment."

Dylan nodded his thanks.

"Now then, my dollings," continued Vilna, "for being such good troupers, I award you with a long weekend. There will be no rehearsal tomorrow." She bowed majestically to the wave of applause that swept the stage, raised her arm in farewell, and crossed to Dylan. "I believe the Rolls Royce awaits us in the alley. Shall we proceed for the exodus?" She inadvertantly took his injured arm.

"Ow!" howled Dylan.

"Oy! You must forgive me."

He looked at her slyly, "I already have." He turned swiftly and called, "Val! Dame Augusta! Our chariot awaits!"

Arm in arm, Lord Carson and Quasimodo were skipping towards the lion's cage.

"Ahroooooooohhhhh!" a deposed king of beasts howled in pain, a paw projecting outward from between the strong iron bars.

"Ouch, ouch, ouch," said Quasimodo, wincing in sympathy with the agonized animal, "he's got a thorn in his paw." He released himself from Lord Carson and began scrambling over the protective barrier that separated the cages from the walk.

"No, no, no, no, no!" cried Lord Carson, his tiny voice trembled with fear, "pussy scratch you!"

"Not me, kiddo, Where I come from it's the other way around." He approached the outstretched paw with caution. "Take it easy, simba old kid. I got lotsa buddies like you back at the circus. I'm a friend. Friend, got it?"

The lion switched his tail back and forth and for a scary moment Quasimodo wasn't sure if the lion was recognizing impending first aid or a second lunch. Quasi whispered, "I'm going to pull out the thorn. It'll be over in a jiffy. I'm coming through to you, right, your majesty?"

Now the tail flicked in circles and Quasimodo was satisfied. Gently, he reached out with his left hand and stroked the back of the paw, and then just as swiftly, his right hand jerked forward, took a firm grip on the thorn, pulled it out—he leapt back as the lion withdrew its paw and licked it.

"There!" cried the hunchbacked boy in drag, "that wasn't so bad, was it?"

The lion purred while Lord Carson hopped up and down and clapped his hands, squealing in joy and admiration. "He your friend now! Harold your friend!"

Quasimodo scrambled back to Lord Carson's side. "Okay, handsome, now lead the way to the crocodile pit."

From a safe distance, a perplexed Mervyn scratched his head. He couldn't believe what he had just seen. A hunchbacked gypsy girl pulling a thorn from a vicious lion's paw.

What a weird tribe.

"No! No!" said Judith Sondergaard in a strangled voice in the spotless kitchen. Gypsy Marie kept peering into her crystal ball.

"It couldn't be worse," muttered Marie. "And by the way, the stock market's going to take another bad dip." Now she looked up. "Under what sign were you born?"

"Cancer."

"Figures." Gypsy's head dropped again and she made three swift passes over the ball. She shook her head sadly and said, "In two words of one syllable each—*oy vay*."

"What is it? Wha do you see?"

"I see terrible things! Terrible! I see the animals on the loose . . . "

"Never!"

"Say listen, whose crystal ball is this? I see flames and destruction and a first-aid kit. And worse—*death!*" Her chair scraped back as she leapt to her feet and leaned across the table looking into Judith Sondergaard's frightened eyes. "It will be like the end of Sodom and Gomorrah! God is coming to destroy, and let me tell you, baby, the way it usually is with Sodom," her finger pointed in the general direction of the zoo, "he's coming in the back way."

"Oh this is nonsense! Nonsense!"

Gypsy Marie wisely sensed the false air of bravado.

The housekeeper stiffened. "I don't understand."

"It came up earlier in the Tarot cards when you drew the hanging man. I interpret him as Sir Vernon."

"No!"

"Sorry, honey, this just isn't your week." Gypsy Marie was now framed in the doorway with her back to the maze and the zoo beyond. "The dark cloud I foresaw hanging over Astoroth House is the cloud of retribution. Even Satan shall turn his back on this house. Let me tell you, he's already planning to cut his losses."

"Get out!" Judith's arm stretched past Marie's nose in a melodramatic gesture, lacking only a snowstorm and an illegitimate baby in the Gypsy's arms. Gypsy Marie shifted the crystal ball from one hand to the other, lifted her well-chiseled head with a dignity and nobility that would have brought drool to a sculptor's lips and left the house.

"Salmonella*aaaaaaaaaa*!"

The shout was matched by the slamming of the door behind her. Once more, Gypsy Marie bellowed the alias.

At the crocodile pit, Quasimodo leapt to his feet.

"Coming, motherrrrrrr!" he shouted, hands cupped to his lavishly lipsticked mouth. Lord Carson tugged at Salmonella's skirt.

"No, no, no. Stay with Carson! Play with Carson!"

"Can't sweetie, Salmonella has to go bye bye with mama."

Tears began forming in little Lord Carson's eyes. "No! No! No! Stay with Carson. Carson loves you!"

Quasimodo said nothing, in expectation of a proposal of marriage but none was forthcoming. He studied the tear-stained eyes holding their special plea of the lonely (which Quasimodo recognized from years of studying his own reflection in a mirror). "Sorry, Carson. I gotta go. Mama knows best."

Carson was clinging to Quasi's right hand. "Stay, stay,

"There is evil beneath this house, I can feel it in my feet, and don't tell me it's bunions because I ain't got any. And the house is growing angry! The house shall tremble and shake until once again it is . . . her hand clenched in a fist was raised above her head, "*stately*!" She lowered her hand and placed it on the ball. "Oh the heat . . . the heat . . . Oh God, feel the heat!"

"That's enough for today," snapped Judith Sondergaard. She was on her feet and had turned her back on Gypsy Marie.

Gypsy Marie straightened, folded her arms, and said, "I'll accept payment now." Judith turned and their eyes met. "There may not be another opportunity."

Once more Judith seemed self-assured with her familiar smirk. She dug into a pocket in her skirt and pulled out some pound notes. She counted three of them and handed them to Gypsy Marie. "That's three pounds. Will that do?"

"It is most satisfactory. I shall collect my child and go. There is sadness at my camp."

"Oh?"

"Our chief's daughter has run away."

"How sad."

"I believe otherwise. I believe she has been . . . abducted."

"Now who would want to kidnap a gypsy girl?"

"Some pervert."

"Let us hope no similar fate befalls your own beloved daughter." Judith Sondergaard was holding open the door that led to the rear of the house. Gypsy Marie sauntered past her jauntily.

"*My* daughter? My blond-haired, hunchbacked beauty? They'd have their hands full with her, let me tell you." Gypsy Marie was now aligned with Judith Sondergaard. "By the by, black beauty. The primrose path you're treading at the moment comes to a dead end."

163

and I show you bad place! Wicked, wicked, forbidden, but I show you, my special friend!"

Quasimodo played it cool. "What bad place?"

"Underneath!" whispered Lord Carson.

"You mean underneath the house?"

Lord Carson's head went up and down rapidly like a cocktail shaker.

"Supposing we get caught?"

"Oh no! Never catch Carson! Carson know secret passageway!"

Gypsy Marie found them. "Come on, Salmonella. Mama's planted her seeds of destruction. Time to go."

"Half a mo', mama. Excuse us a second, Carson." He drew Gypsy Marie to one side for a hurried conference. Gypsy Marie listened and stroked her chin.

"I wonder," she muttered under her breath, "I wonder if we dare."

A threatening sky hung over London shortly before six that evening. Max Van Larsen hurried along a platform at Charing Cross Station looking for an empty second-class compartment. Three cars past the buffet he found one. He climbed in, slammed the door shut behind him, placed his weekend case on the overhead rack, and studied himself in the small, square mirror on the wall. He was satisfied his thick glasses and hat pulled tightly about his ears would sustain his disguise. Max sat, crossed his legs, and waited impatiently until he heard the station master's whistle which signalled the imminent departure of the train to Punting-on-the-Thames.

The train trembled as the wheels meshed and the departure was underway. Max exhaled with relief and groped in his jacket pocket for cigarettes. When the cigarette was lit and the match extinguished, Max shut his eyes and leaned back. In his mind, Sylvia Plotkin metamorphosed from an ectoplasmic cloud. Brave, beautiful, pugnacious Sylvia. How magnificently she'd been carrying out his careful instructions. How gallantly she discounted danger to prove she was a vixen worthy of such a fox as Van Larsen. How carefully she had assimilated what information he could provide and then convinced him Edna would be a valuable asset on the team.

The team! Van Larsen, Sylvia, Edna, Vilna, Roberts, Gypsy Marie, and Quasimodo. Truly an all-star cast.

There'd been a last-minute conversation with Sylvia before the Rolls Royce arrived to pick them up at the Dorchester. He'd briefly been given the details of her and Edna's luncheons. At last they'd been able to utilize the information he'd given them about Joe Gordon's past relationship to Evelyn Blair.

Like a slide projector, there was a click in his brain and Evelyn Blair's face replaced Sylvia's. It wasn't as clear as his beloved's because he had met the Blair woman only once, when she had interviewed him a few days after his earlier arrival in London. He'd given her a brief hour before his departure with Joe Gordon and Madame Vilna for Astoroth House and while in his mind the reporter's hawklike features were hazy, the unique clarionlike voice was as clear as though she was talking this moment. It was in the car that Joe Gordon had told him about meeting Evelyn in the Far East some two decades earlier—and described a beauty that had gradually been warped by bitterness and emotional defeat.

He remembered Joe, sitting between him and a silent Madame Vilna in the back seat of the Rolls, told him of Evelyn defecting from husband and son, and then Joe defecting from Evelyn for the woman who was to die an alcoholic. Yet Evelyn Blair had apparently forgiven Joe. She met Lisa Gordon and became a second mother to her.

Van Larsen barely heard the sliding door to the

passageway open and then gently shut. Eyes closed, he was completely absorbed in his own thoughts, completely fascinated by the red light that was now flashing vividly behind Evelyn Blair's unclear features. He suddenly remembered when the chauffeur's hands had slipped from the steering wheel and Madame Vilna shrieked *"Guttenyoo!"* as they narrowly avoided sideswiping an oncoming motorcyclist.

He opened his eyes in time to notice a quarter inch of cigarette ash about to drop on his trousers. He quickly moved his hand to the ashtray in the door and then settled back again, at last noticing he was no longer alone in the compartment.

The voice he heard was a buzz saw attacking a redwood.

"Welcome back, Mr. Van Larsen."

Max recognized the face sitting opposite him and said, "Speak of the devil."

Rom Magyar was gnawing morosely at a mutton leg when he saw Gypsy Marie's wagon returning to the camp. His eyes searched the empty seat next to Gypsy Marie and then watched as the woman nonchalantly descended and sashayed towards her tent.

"Woman!" he shouted, "wait!"

Gypsy Marie's hand froze on the tent flap as Rom Magyar flung the bone aside and rushed to her.

"Your daughter?" he cried, "Where is your daughter?"

"I left her to frolic with Lord Carson."

He stared at her dumbfounded, his tongue paralyzed.

"Believe me, Rom Magyar," said Gypsie Marie confidently, "I know what I'm doing. I told you, you must trust me. Do not look so bewildered. There is no madness to my method. Join me in my tent and we'll kill a few martinis."

Joseph Gordon's guests in the Rolls Royce were in unusually high spirits, thanks to the luxurious car's well-stocked bar. Gordon shared the back of the car with Edna, Sylvia, Madame Vilna, and Dame Augusta. Dylan Wake and Lady Valerie were in front with Harry Sanders. Liquor had seemingly numbed memories of the previous day's murders and Dylan's unfortunate experience at White City. For over an hour Sylvia had wittily regaled them with her courtship of Max Van Larsen and the various cases in which she, Edna, and Madame Vilna had been involved.

When Sylvia finally seemed about to flag, Madame Vilna caught the conversational ball and convulsed them with anecdotes of her years as a great star of the Yiddish theatre. She leapt from memory to memory like a mountain goat.

She leaned forward and poked a preoccupied Dylan in the back of the neck. "Pay attention! I am talking now of the young Muni Weisenfreund, who is perhaps more familiar to you as the late Paul Muni! I saw in *him* what I sometimes see in you and see how he ascended the heights! *The heights!* Of course now he is in heaven, which is as far as you can go. But ah! When he and I stole scenes from each other in *Zetzen Zie Gicher, Du Fahrdrayst Der Schiffel*, which is perhaps more familiar to you as *Major Barbara*, that was fireworks, I tell you, fireworks! Darling Joseph, how clever of you to stock your automobile with slivovitz. Yes, I would adore another *soupcon!*"

Dame Augusta squinted out the window. "I think a storm's about to break."

"It's been hanging over us since we left London," said Lady Valerie.

In the distance loomed Astoroth House.

"That's Astoroth House up ahead," Joe Gordon told Sylvia and Edna.

"How majestic!" gasped Sylvia.

And then Edna rumbled, "'Last night I dreamt I saw

Manderley again.' "

"How clever you are," said Dame Augusta, "it's been compared before to Daphne DuMaurier's creation."

In the distance, they saw lightning flash over Astoroth House.

"I hope Judith's shutting the windows," said Lady Valerie blandly.

Edna's hand moved and found Sylvia, and for a charming moment, to Joe Gordon they looked like frightened little girls, orphans of the storm.

Esmeralda couldn't believe her ears.

"Somebody's calling my name!

"Here! Here!" she shouted as she leapt from the cot and rushed towards the door, only to be brought up short by her brutal shackles. She heard a scramble outside her door. Two hands wrapped themselves around the two bars in the aperture of the door and Quasimodo's face appeared.

"Hi, there," he said gingerly, "I'm Gypsy Marie's girl, Salmonella. How they treating you?"

"Awful! I've had an injection that makes me feel very strange and dangerous and right now it's wearing off, I think, which is why I am coherent. Get me out of here!"

"In time, in time, in time! We can't rush things. But don't worry, the cavalry's coming."

"Esmeralda's face lit up like a dirty bulb. "Soldiers!"

"Relax! Don't worry! And for the time being, play dumb!"

Little did he realize he'd assigned her an easy task.

"I'm frightened! I have heard terrible things here! Last night I heard girls screaming!"

"Three cells down," Quasimodo informed her, "two hippy hopheads. Yuppie campers. Missing since last week. All doped up and no place to go. Gotta go now,

I think Carson's back is killing him."

Little Lord Carson was on his hands and knees outside the door to Esmeralda's cell bolstering Quasimodo.

"Head hurt," he whimpered, "head hurt . . . hurt awful!" His hands flew to his scar and Quasimodo lost his balance.

Esmeralda heard a scurrying of feet and then Quasimodo's voice called, "Hey Carson, come back! Hey Carson wait up . . . I don't know my way out of here!"

The sky darkened, lightning flashed, thunder rumbled, and the storm descended. The countryside was inundated by torrential rain and buffeting winds. A protecting canvas cover did not totally obscure Nick Hastings' red Volvo parked in the Astoroth House driveway as the Rolls Royce pulled in. Edna nudged Sylvia, who nodded abstractedly, her line of vision having reached the open doorway and the imposing figure of Judith Sondergaard.

"Ah!" cried Madame Vilna, "there stands the faithful housekeeper!" She rolled down the window on her side and shouted through the storm, "So where's umbrellas, you *schwartzer cholleryah*?"

Black curse, thought Sylvia in a literal translation. *Black witch*.

From behind Judith Sondergaard emerged the three zoo attendants with large black umbrellas.

What ugly looking brutes, thought Sylvia.

"Di-*vine*, thought Edna.

"Let's go!" shouted Joe Gordon.

Amanda Brush was in the study shutting the windows against the storm when she saw the local taxi pulling in at the front of the vicarage.

"Vicar!" she shouted.

Oscar Treble has already heard the familiar motor and held the front door ajar, eyes squinting against the buffeting winds and rain. He discerned Max from the back seat paying the driver and wondered, who was the woman with him? But only Max emerged with his case, leaping the few feet from taxi to door. The cab drove away with the woman. The vicar stood to one side as Max squeezed into the vestibule.

The vicar pressed the door shut and then turned to Max with outstretched arms.

"My son, my son. Alive and well. I can barely believe my eyes. Amanda! Come take Father Green's suitcase!"

Amanda Brush entered and her chin dropped. "Father Who?"

"Amanda, my dear," said the vicar amiably, "a little surprise we've arranged for tomorrow night's revels. I can trust you to share our secret, can't I, Amanda?" Amanda recognized the tone of voice and nodded gravely. "and Amanda, one word of Mr. Van Larsen's presence to anyone . . . *anyone* . . . and I shall reveal the shame of your birth!"

Amanda cringed and then picked up Van Larsen's case. In a trembling voice she told him, "You're in the Saint Francis of Assisi room, third door to your left. It's where the birds gather in the morning."

"Thank you, Amanda," said Max as she began ascending the stairs, and then the vicar beckoned him to the study.

The vicar poured drinks while Max warmed himself at the roaring fireplace, and then the vicar sat at his desk under the multi-pinned map.

"I must say, Max," said the vicar with twinkling eyes, "I'm beginning to feel like a character in one of my own thrillers. What excitement, all this! But Mr. Roberts has told me so little, what exactly *is* planned for tomorrow night?"

A trim black Volkswagon pulled up at the Marksman's Inn at the edge of the village of Punting-on-the-Thames. Two of its doors opened disgorging three men carrying overnight bags and gun cases. They plunged through the raging storm into the welcoming warmth of the lobby. The innkeeper, a Mr. Trevis Otis, rushed from behind his desk to greet the new arrivals.

"Mr. Roberts, I thought you'd never make it through this storm!" He greeted the two others. "Mr. Willoughby? Mr. Simmons?" The detectives nodded. "Welcome, welcome, there are hot toddies for you in the lounge. I'll have your things taken to your rooms. Terrible storm! Worst we've had in years, I reckon. Doesn't look like much hunting for you tomorrow."

"Oh," said Roberts as he reached into his jacket for his pipe, "I wouldn't be too sure about that."

The hunting room of Astoroth House also had a welcome warmth emanating from its blazing fireplace, where the household and its guests were relaxing with drinks and hors d'ouevres. Sylvia had managed to whisper to Edna, "Don't touch any mushroom dip." But Edna was too overwhelmed by the decor.

"My God," she gasped, "Gobelin tapestries, Heppel-white furniture, the wall covered with original Turners, and these *rugs*!"

Edna was then fascinated by a wall of antique weapons: muskets, crossbows, and, to her astonishment, a slingshot.

"Lord Carson's," explained Judith Sondergaard sweetly. "As soon as you've had your refreshments, you'll be assigned your rooms. Dinner will be a bit delayed this evening. There was a bit of a struggle with the fatted calf."

Sir Vernon asked Judith with concern, "Where's Lord Carson? I haven't seen him all afternoon."

"Come to think of it," said Judith, "I haven't seen him myself since he went romping in the zoo this afternoon with that gypsy girl, Salmonella."

Three sets of ears warmed to the gypsy girl's name and Madame Vilna attacked a plate of smoked oysters. Sylvia, joining Madame Vilna, inquired anxiously, "Any lox?"

Dylan Wake stood by himself staring into the fireplace where Lady Valerie joined him. "What's wrong with you? You've been a brown study since lunch."

There was a knock at the door and Harry Sanders entered and crossed to Joseph Gordon. "The car's in the garage, Mr. Gordon. Will there be anything else?"

Dylan Wake glared across the room at him when one of the zoo attendants, Mervyn, wearing ill-fitting livery, appeared in the doorway.

"Miz Ee-velyn Blah," he announced.

"Blair," she snapped as she pushed past him into the room. "Sorry I'm late, but I gave somebody a lift in my taxi to the vicarage."

Edna shot a look at Sylvia who shot one at Vilna who shot one at Edna.

"Filthy night out," bazooka'd Evelyn Blair, "who do I have to kiss to get a glass of sherry?"

Before she could speak any further, there was the weird, eerie sound of a badly oiled wheel turning. The startled group's attention was drawn to a huge sideboard against a far wall of the room.

"Goodness!" cried Edna, "that sideboard is moving!"

"Oy!" gasped Madame vilna, "it brings back with total recall a terrifying moment in *Immitzer Vill Essen der Fagele*, which is perhaps more familiar to you as *The Cat And The Canary*!"

Sylvia stifled a scream as the sideboard slowly propelled outwardly in an arc. A panel of the wall slid to one side and into the room hurled a screaming boy clutching his head yelling, "Hurt! Hurt! Head hurt! Hurt awful!"

"Carson!" shouted Lord Vernon.

Lord Carson halted in his tracks as his eyes swept the room. And then, as though besieged by invisible demons, he pointed a frail finger at the group and screamed, "There! *There*! Bad One! *Bad One*!"

Harry Sanders didn't even flinch.

CHAPTER
twelve

"Well-mannered young men don't point."

All eyes were on Sylvia Plotkin. The gentle admonishment was accompanied by the faint smile familiar to her students back at Robert F. Wagner High School—the deceptive prelude to the announcement that she was about to collect and destroy their crack. Lord Carson lowered his head abashedly, his excruciating pain apparently numbed by the anodyne in Sylvia's voice.

Nick Hastings, who apparently knew his way around Astoroth House, had pulled a lever that sent the sliding panel and sideboard back into place. It was the first time Edna became aware of his presence and realized he'd been hidden by a wing chair facing the fireplace from the time they had entered the room.

Sylvia crossed to Lord Carson and patted his head. "What hurts?"

He looked up slowly and was inundated by the warmth emanating from Sylvia.

"Here."

Sylvia leaned over and kissed the scar. "There, I've kissed the hurt away. Isn't it all gone now?"

Lord Carson impulsively flung his arms around her waist and gave her a gentle hug. "You my friend! I take you exploring!"

"Not now, darling," said Lady Valerie, "time to wash and dress for dinner."

Lord Carson still clung to Sylvia. She heard his whispering, "Explore later, yes?"

"It's a date," replied Sylvia *sotto voce*.

Judith Sondergaard took Lord Carson's hand and began to lead him from the room.

"I forgot something," he suddenly said, his face screwed up with perplexity.

"What did you forget?" asked Judith sounding like crashing timber.

"I forgot." He pulled his hand away and skipped out of the room.

Joseph Gordon dismissed Harry Sanders while Sir Vernon said "Urrmph" and turned to Edna with interest. "That terrible scar," said Edna, "what happened to the poor boy?"

"Struck by a blunt instrument several years ago. He has severe brain damage. Would you believe he's in his twenties?"

"What a tragedy."

"He's wasting away. He grows smaller by the week. He was a brilliant boy, wasn't he, Nick?"

Nick nodded and Edna remembered that he and Lord Carson had been university students together. Then she wondered, was that a flash of fear cutting across those laser eyes? Is this a flash of fear illuminating my intestines? She heard a noise like splintering wood and realized Dame Augusta was speaking.

176

"Now, for a tour of the ancestral gallery." She favored Evelyn Blair with a mincing smile. "Would you care to join Edna, Sylvia, and myself?"

"I'd be delighted," said Evelyn. "I always enjoy getting to the bottom of things."

Dame Augusta led the ladies from the room as Lady Valerie whispered urgently to Dylvan, "What's wrong with you?"

"What's right?" he snapped and moved away from her as he saw Sir Vernon approach. Sir Vernon drew his wife to one side.

"Was it necessary?"

"Was what necessary?"

"Greystoke, Nelly Locke."

"Obviously, someone thought so."

"It was madness!"

"I won't argue. You're the authority. It was your descent from grace that drove us to this."

"Oh Val . . . Val," he pleaded, "when did the magic go out of our lives?"

"Honest to Satan, if you don't stop reading Jackie Collins . . ."

Lonely like a cloud, Quasimodo cautiously wandered through the vast underground labyrinth. *Oh boy, oh boy, oh boy! I'll never find my way out of this place. Torture chambers and an underground river and cells and more cells and dungeons and everything that goes with it except Vincent Price. What was that? I heard somebody groan? Where? Which direction?*

He was standing in the center of a narrow, seemingly endless passageway.

There it goes again. It sounds like it's coming from under me. Carefully, he tested the floor with his foot and felt the iron bars of a grating. Cautiously, he knelt and listened again.

Definitely from down here.

"Pssst!" he hissed through the grating.

A feeble voice with a heavy Far Eastern accent inquired, "Is that you, Allah?"

"I'm a friend," whispered Quasimodo, "who are you?"

"Pandit Perski," came a feeble response.

"What are you doing down there?"

"What I have been doing for lo, the past two moons, praying. My knees grow weary and my rug is frayed. Have you a compass by any chance? I'm a bit confused as to the direction of Mecca."

"How'd you get down there?"

"I was pushed. First, they took my money and then the effigy of the God whom I worship. Ay, they stole my bread and Buddha."

"Are you an illegal immigrant?"

"Hush your mouth. It is more polite to describe me as an uninvited guest. We came by way of the great ocean and then by night up the river that leads to a hidden landing place behind the zoo of this accursed house. But something has gone wrong. I overheard something has gone wrong, and I am told there is a plan to kill us by flooding this section. Help us, help us!"

"How many of you are there?"

"We are twelve."

"Okay. If I find my way out of here, I'll bring help!"

"Allah and Buddha go with you!"

Quasimodo scampered away. *Oh boy, oh boy, oh boy! I've found all the proof Max needs. I've found it all! All I have to do is find him and lead him here and . . . how?*

The magnificent Mayhew ancestral portraits lined the walls of the imposing great hall on the second floor of Astoroth House. Dame Augusta was now paused beneath a portrait of two unhappy-looking women painted facing each other. Dame Augusta informed her guests, "These are the twin daughters of scornful Carl, the Contumacious. As you will notice, the one on the left looks sated and the one on the right looks cowardly. They were known from left to right as Jacqueline, the Jaded and Jane, the Jaundiced. Suspected of being witches," Dame Augusta attributed a sudden intake of breath to Sylvia Plotkin, "They fled to Spain where the Inquisition got them."

"Out of the frying pan into the fire, eh?" offered Edna.

Dame Augusta had moved on to another portrait. "This imposing gentleman was an inventor. Among other things, the chisel and the screwdriver are attributed to him. He was called Morris, the Monotonous."

Edna whispered with boredom to Sylvia, "I'd run amuck if I was licensed."

"Courage. There's only about another six dozen portraits to go."

"Din-dins in fifteen minutes," Amanda Brush announced from the study doorway to the vicar and Max and then disappeared.

From his easy chair facing the vicar behind his desk, Max had a clear view of the map and its vari-colored pins. "Which is Black Bernard's latest route?"

"Ah, you remember!" said the delighted Mr. Treble.

"It was a most diverting tea that Saturday, Mr. Treble."

Oscar Treble leaned forward with a serious expression. "What will happen to my friends at Astoroth House? Surely they are merely dupes, innocent pawns."

Max studied the drink he was holding as he spoke. "At first, perhaps. But they had time to give the consequences serious thought and back away from it if they so desired. But I'm afraid they were too consumed by greed."

"But they are *aristocracy*."

"There are bad apples in every barrel."

"I suppose the village is swarming with police."

Max smiled. "We're not unprepared."

"Ah me! Ah me! Poor Augusta." He was toying with a pencil. "I've known her quite a few years."

"Really? Before you were assigned here two years ago?"

"Oh dearie me, yes. We first met some ten years ago when I was doing missionary work in Bangkok and she was touring with a small but quite clever Shakespearian group. She'd fallen on very hard times. Lady Valerie was with her."

"And Dylan Wake by any chance?"

"That scapegrace! That dreadful scalliwag! He was in his teens then, playing minor roles and causing major havoc. I tried to convert him but he scoffed. He is truly Godless, that young man. He was in scrape after scrape until half the city was chafing from them. It was because of him Dame Augusta was forced to cut short their stay in Bangkok."

"What happened?"

"Oh dear, oh dear. I cannot breach that confidence! After all, I *am* a man of the cloth and he *did* confess to me."

"You helped him out of the situation?"

"Helped *them*. For Augusta's sake. For dear Augusta's sake."

"Where was Irving her husband?"

"He died shortly before the tour. Augusta needed to get away and so organized the troupe which unfortunately was booked by a rather unscrupulous agent. It was a sad time for all of them." There was a faraway look in his eye. "I remember the night they departed Bangkok with a caravan of friendly merchants making for Persia. They'd hidden all day without food or water, poor souls. Finally, under cover of the caravan, a resident houri gave them some uncooked vegetables. My last sight of Augusta

180

was her holding a gnarled carrot and swearing to the others, 'As God is my witness, I'll never go hungry again.'"

"You lost track of the Mayhews after that?"

The pencil lead broke and the vicar laid it aside. "Augusta was instrumental in bringing me to Punting-on-the-Thames, so you see, I owe her a great deal."

"Have you thought of retirement? You must have a comfortable income from your books."

The vicar laughed. "My dear Max, few thriller writers die rich." His fingers were pressed together. "But I do pray I spend my remaining years in comfort."

"I'm with you there, Vicar," said Max as he helped himself to another drink, "I'd like to retire to someplace like Switzerland."

"Ah, Switzerland!"

Max crossed to a window and drew the curtain aside and looked at the raging storm outside. "I'm in my forties now. I feel myself slowing down. I've had time to think after my unpleasant experience at Astoroth House. I'd like to make a big bundle, get myself a charming chalet, and who knows . . ." he was now facing the vicar, "get some of those treatments at the Rejuvenation Center."

"Oh, you're still much too young for that." He looked at the door to the kitchen anxiously. "What*ever* could be the delay in dinner? I'm absolutely famished! Aren't you?"

Amanda Brush screamed.

Max sprinted to the kitchen with the vicar waddling behind him. They found Amanda Brush threatening a drenched Gypsy Marie Rachmaninoff with a teflon frying pan. The kitchen door was open and rain was gushing in over the floor.

"Max!"

"Gypsy Marie! What's wrong?"

"Qua—" she caught herself in time. "Salmonella, it's Salmonella." Her eyes darted suspiciously from Amanda to the vicar. "I would have words with you in private."

"Amanda!" snapped the vicar, "shut the door before we're forced to build an ark!" Amanda obeyed instantly. "Max, my study is at your disposal." He clucked his tongue in Gypsy Marie's direction. "You poor woman, you're soaked to the skin."

Gypsy Marie's eyes narrowed. "You are very observant, vicar."

The vicar bowed and pointed to the study, "Your obedient observant."

Madame Vilna was dressing for dinner when there came a knock at her door. She reached for her lavish purple bathrobe, slipped it on, and yodeled, *"Entrez!"*

Dylan Wake entered and shut the door behind him. There was a crash of thunder and a flash of lightening and she heard him say, "Help me."

Vilna was all concern. "What is wrong, my misbegotten?"

"Oh Jesus, I'm frightened!" He hurled himself across the room, fell on his knees, and tightly embraced her legs, which were as firm and solidly planted as tree trunks.

"You are perhaps having trouble with your lines?" she murmured as she stroked his thick red hair.

He sank back on his haunches and looked up. "No jokes, me old darlin'. No jokes. you stabbed me last night, didn't you?"

"It was necessary."

"I know. I forgive you."

"You are very gallant."

"Valerie's told me why she thinks you did it. Someone Valerie thinks she saw with Roberts."

"Such as?"

"Max Van Larsen."

Vilna strode slowly to the dressing table and sat. She studied her face in the mirror. "Van Larsen is in a sanitorium in America."

Dylan bit his lip and then slowly got to his feet. "They're closing in on us, aren't they?"

Vilna was busily applying mascara to her eyelashes with graceful strokes. "As my fifth husband, Marcus something-or-another, said to me as he leapt from our penthouse window, 'Vilna, all good things must come to an end.' He wore his best suit."

"Help me. Please."

She turned around wth an effort and the pitiable sight filled her heart with empathy. "What would you have me do?"

"Get me to Max."

Vilna's voice grew stern. "Lady Valerie sent you here."

"No! No!" He had crossed the room and was kneeling again. Vilna looked like Catherine of Russia giving audience to a serf. "Greystoke's murder was one thing . . . but *Nelly*! Don't you see? I'm *next*."

"*You*? Ooowah, ha, ha, ha, ha, ha!" Her wattles jiggled merrily as her head wig-wagged. Dylan winced as the palm of her hand fell flat on his head, like the gesture of an unspoken benediction. "But I assume you lead a charmed life! Did you not survive that stomping? Aren't there others who have harbored hatred towards you, and still you survive? The man you told me about, the one who poured money into your career, did he not attempt to kill you?"

"I want to open as Hamlet!"

"Aha! Once an actor always an actor!" She pushed him aside, arose, and crossed to her purse to rummage for a cigarette. "Whatever you have to tell Max, tell me."

"You wouldn't be safe."

"My dear buddy boy," said Vilna as she applied a lighter to the cigarette now jutting from the corner of her mouth, "Vilna is invincible. She has survived three wars, eight husbands and an occasional hostile critic." She tossed the lighter onto the bed and blew a perfect smoke ring. "For example, the late George Jean Nathan was most unappreciative of my Riffker in *Ich Doff Derhogernan Mein Mann*, which is perhaps more familiar to you as Regina in *The Little Foxes*."

She now stood against a window with the rain pelting the panes and a tree outside bending under the fury of the wind.

"Tell me everything, Dylan. If it would help to relax you, I give you leave to throw youself at my feet."

Outside Vilna's door, Nick Hastings knelt peering through the keyhole. Then he pressed his ear to the door and listened. He did not hear a door on the opposite side of the corridor open a crack.

Sylvia was about to look for the dining room and inquire about dinner when she opened the door and saw Hastings eavesdropping. Very gently, she shut the door again and turned to Edna who was clamping an earring to an earlobe. Sylvia put a finger to her lips and Edna shrugged inquisitively. Sylvia motioned Edna to the door, cautiously re-opened it, and Edna pressed an eye to the crack. Gently, Sylvia closed the door again and Edna motioned her to the other side of the room.

"What do you suppose Vilna's up to in there?" Edna whispered.

"Maybe he's watching her getting dressed."

"*Vilna?*"

"Edna darling," said Sylvia, "my mother always said, 'There's a cover for every pot.' "

"I think it's outrageous!" Edna seethed, "I'm going out there and tell him so!"

"Wait! Edna, for crying out loud *don't*!"

Her plea fell on deaf ears. Edna pulled open the door and houted, "Now see here—!"

Nick Hastings was gone. Sylvia was looking over Edna's shoulder and was about to say something when Vilna's door opened and Dylan Wake emerged, Edna hastily shut their door.

"I *don't* believe it!" gasped Edna.

In his room at the Marksman's Inn, Detective-Inspector Channing Roberts held a phone to his ear and bit down on the stem of his pipe. Max was speaking from the other end.

"That is definitely most unfortunate," said Roberts, "but we don't dare move in on them now. Damn it, Max, we need evidence—living proof! It's *got* to wait until tomorrow night."

Max and Gypsy Marie were alone in the vicar's study. He clutched the phone tightly and his face was red with anger and anxiety.

"We know they won't stop at murder, Chan! If they've got Quasi, they might torture the poor kid. And then what happens to Sylvia, Edna, Vilna . . . !"

"Steady old boy," he heard Roberts say, "all were warned of the dangers before joining the enterprise."

Gypsy Marie paced the room while the argument continued. *Torture. Quasimodo.* Beads of perspiration reflected on her forehead while she steadily stroked a rabbit's paw she carried in her skirt pocket. I foresaw doom there, she was thinking, I told Sondergaard the house would tremble. Is it *I* who is predestined to shake its foundations? She reached Max and grabbed his arm. "Wait."

"Hold it, Chan, Gypsy Marie wants to say something."

"Cover the mouthpiece." He covered it. "They will not harm Quasi. He is disguised as Salmonella. At the very worst, he is incarcerated alongside the smelly Esmeralda. They will mark Quasi for shipment abroad along with the others. They may have doped him and I'll have to see him through the period of cold turkey, but that is all. Mr. Roberts is right. We musn't jump the gun. If I, his mother, am willing to wait, then you must wait too."

Max sighed. "You're a wise woman, Marie."

"They don't come any smarter, sweetie." She laughed vivaciously. "So, how come I'm still single?"

"Chan? forget it. Marie's willing to go along. Sorry I pushed the panic button." He almost added, "I would die without Sylvia Plotkin," but instead said, "Speak to you in the morning."

Roberts hung up the phone and addressed Willoughby and Simmons who were in his room sharing a drink. "I'm a bit worried about Max. Yes, quite a bit worried."

"You're much too rash and impetuous, Nick!" stormed Lady Valerie in her private sitting room, flouncing in a St. Laurent hostess gown. Curlicues of smoke from the cigarette projecting from the ivory holder she was waving attacked Dame Augusta who coughed and grasped her lace handkerchief.

"Valerie is right," Dame Augusta managed to say between coughs, "earlier rashness and impetuosity on your part have cost us dearly!"

"Meaning?" Hastings towered over her like a blond Mephistopheles.

"You know bloody well what I mean. I'm an old woman but not an old fool. There are other ways of taking care of Dylan Wake. What's wrong with you, Valerie? You look like a cocker spaniel bitch about to abort."

"I could just *strangle* Dylan!"

"There's a less violent method," suggested Hastings smoothly.

"Oh shut up, Nicholas," commanded Dame Augusta.

"Eliminating Dylan means eliminating Vilna, and I've grown rather fond of the monster. I abhor *murder*." She was undismayed by a mental flash of her late Irving and instead chose to tap a foot impatiently. "It has to look accidental."

"What does?" asked Lady Valerie.

"Dylan." Her audience as transfixed. "Tomorrow night during the ritual."

"If the rain keeps up, we'll be washed out," said Valerie.

"We move to the cellar sacrificial room. Tell Judith to get it dusted just in case. Valerie . . ."

"Yes?" eagerly.

"We haven't done the transmigration of soul bit in months."

"Oh Auntie, what a capital idea!"

"Thank you dear, you *are* nice. Dylan always throws himself into that with spirit. I'll mix the necessary concoction myself in the greenhouse tomorrow. You work it out with him. He won't suspect a thing. And if perchance my hand slips and I mistake the nightshade for the rosemary, ah well . . . by then Plan X will be in operation. Which reminds me, strange we haven't heard from himself this evening. Valerie, what is *wrong* with you?"

"Oh, it's nothing, nothing." She tamped her cigarette in an ashtray while Nick Hastings folded his arms and smiled like an adder.

"It's Dylan," he said.

Valerie's eyes met his. "This too shall pass, you bastard."

"All tucked in comfy?" Judith Sondergaard asked Lord Carson as his head settled against the pillow.

"All comfy."

"Shall I tell you a bedtime story?"

"Oh *yes*."

Judith sat on the bed and stroked his hand. "Well once

upon a time there was this psychopathic killer named Jack The Ripper. . . ."

A trapdoor!
Quasimodo's lighter flickered as he held it over his head and stared at the ceiling.
Now how do I reach it?
He was in a dank, damp corridor and the ceiling was fringed with cobwebs. He lowered the lighter and looked for something to stand on. He espied a filthy ladder.
Ah!
When the ladder was propped against the wall, Quasimodo carefully ascended each rung before bringing his full weight on it.
Careful, Quasi, he cautioned himself, *careful. You can't be too sure there isn't a new danger past that trapdoor. Be very careful.*

He tested the trapdoor with one hand. It didn't budge.
Stuck. He cursed under his breath and tried again. dust showered down into his face. He found a handkerchief in his skirt, wiped his face, and attacked the door again. Slowly it began to give. He climbed another rung and stuck his head through the trapdoor.
He saw the rain and felt the wind and heard thunder. Through the bars and Quasi felt a sticky warmth on his face and realized he was being licked.
Gently he whispered, "That you, Carson?"

Coffee and brandy were served in the Crusader's Lounge of Astoroth House. The dinner had been delicious. Conversation had been confined to small talk. Witchcraft, thought Sylvia over dessert, has been pointedly avoided, and it's just as well. She was tired and in no mood for black banter. But if a girl doesn't watch her step, she can be swept into a fatal whirlpool by the undercurrents in this room. She noticed Dylan Wake barely touched his food and drank too much wine; Joseph Gordon perspired a great deal and rarely took his eyes from Lady Valerie; Sir Vernon affably engaged Edna in conversation and kept insisting he wasn't the one to compile a new medical dictionary; Evelyn Blair directed an occasional snide remark at Nick Hastings who kept his cool. Amazingly, no reference was made by anyone to the Blair bombshell published that morning.

Yes, decided Sylvia, there are undercurrents and even Vilna looks like a cat who's swallowed the canary.

Sylvia stared at her brandy with distaste and stifled a yawn. So how's my Max, she wondered, maybe playing a game of chess with the vicar? And has Mr. Roberts already gone beddy-bye or is he polishing his hunting rifle? She glanced at her wristwatch, stifled another yawn and announced, "Me for bed. It's way past my time."

Evelyn Blair said with a simper, "Party poop."

"I'll be up in a few minutes," Edna said to Sylvia and returned to her marathon conversation with Sir Vernon.

Judith Sondergaard appeared in the doorway and said to the approaching Sylvia, "Off to bed so soon?"

"Afraid so," said Sylvia affably, "I'm not the girl I used to be."

Judith smiled and her voice crackled "Night night." Then her eyes moved to Sir Vernon and Edna and narrowed with jealousy.

Sylvia was hunting for her bedroom when a door opened and she heard, "Pssssst!" Sylvia, startled, turned and saw Lord Carson.

"Young man, young man, you should be asleep."

Lord Carson laughed. "Carson never sleep. Carson *explores.*" He ran to her and took her hand tightly. "Carson take you exploring *now.*"

"It's too late, sweetheart."

"No, no, no, no, no!" He stamped a foot and was petulant. "Carson remember what he forget. He forget Salmonella."

Sylvia was no longer tired. "What about her?"

Carson told her and Sylvia went white. "All right, Carson, we'll go exploring." She squared her shoulders. "Lead on."

CHAPTER
thirteen

Evelyn Blair was the next to retire, followed by Joseph Gordon, and she wasn't too surprised when he invited himself to her room for a nightcap. She studied him as she measured out cognacs and thought to herself that time *was* the great equalizer. I needed him once, now he needs me. As she crossed to him with the snifters, she inquired amiably, "What's on your mind, Joe? You certainly didn't invite yourself in to make a pass. That's past."

Gently, he swirled the liqueur as his hands warmed the snifter. "Come into my parlor said the spider to the fly." He looked up and watched her sit in an easy chair opposite him. "If I'd known you'd been invited this weekend, I'd have done everything possible to dissuade you."

"You wouldn't have been successful, you know that. They won't do anything to me, they don't dare. And it'll make a dandy follow-up story to the one I published this morning." She crossed her legs reminding Gordon that some of her anatomy was still in good shape. "I thought you looked rather astonished when I made my entrance." Her voice flattened. "Is Lisa alive?"

He'd forgotten she was a mistress at the swift uppercut.

"Well, is she?"

"You're so sure I know where she is."

"Very sure. Your demeanor the past month has hardly been that of a frantic father."

"Wasn't sending for Max frantic enough?"

"No, it was just further evidence of your usual clever thinking. I've been a party to your frantic S.O.S.'s before, remember? Except Max did his job too well and had to be eliminated. Where's Lisa?"

"She's alive."

"*Where*?"

He slammed the brandy glass down on an end table and it proved sturdier then the timbre of his voice which took on an unbecoming whine. "She'll stay alive if you and the others get the hell out of here."

"You're an ass, Joseph. It's much too late for that and you know it. It's curtains for Astoroth House and our hosts are being brazen about it because they're dead sure of a safe getaway. What I'm interested in knowing is, are *you* joining the farewell tour?"

"What the hell are you insinuating?"

"You shouldn't wear such tight collars. You never stop tugging at them." She was enjoying herself immensely. "By Christ, I hate men." Her voice went up an octave. "You and Valerie, that's what I'm insinuating!"

"Ridiculous!"

"Any bets?"

He slumped deeper into his chair.

Evelyn uncrossed her legs and leaned forward. "Lisa suspected as much and told me. Joe, did she really phone you the night she disappeared?"

"Bitch!"

"I thought not. Did she ever get here?"

"*Bitch!*"

"I thought not. You realize, of course, I'm not alone in that theory." She sipped the brandy and grimaced. "Jesus, I hate cognac." She set the glass aside. "Where's Lisa?"

"Abroad."

"*Where?*"

"Where she's safe, that's where." He was on his feet and glaring down at her with menace. "I had her removed for her own safety. *Now* will you pack your bag and get out of here?"

"It's raining too hard. And I don't like your story, Joe. It needs revision."

"Up you."

"Never dwell in the past dear. If she's safe, why send for Van Larsen? Shame on you, Joe, you always could smell out a good story and then tell it— " and *click* went her mind. Slowly she arose and they were face to face. "Why you son of a bitch, so *that's* what you're all about!" She pointed a finger under his nose. "You've been hoarding this damn story for *yourself*! And that's why Lisa—'

"May no longer be safe, thanks to *you*!"

Harry Sanders' room was above the garage adjoining the zoo. Shortly after midnight, reclining on his bed reading a copy of *Playboy*, he began wondering if he was going mad. Through the fury of the storm outside he could swear he was hearing Renata Tebaldi singing. He flung the magazine aside, arose, and crossed to the window overlooking the zoo. He shaded his eyes and squinted through the dirt-streaked pane but saw nothing but cages and covered stalls.

Harry had learned to appreciate opera during his most recent incarceration, having shared a cell with a third-rate tenor who was serving twenty years for manslaughter (he stabbed the conductor who had been pacing *The Barber of Seville* too slowly).

Harry poked around his left ear and then shook his head.

I *must* be going bonkers. That is a very, very familiar aria I hear. Damn!

He pulled his mackintosh from its hanger, put it on quickly after a brief struggle with an inverted sleeve, found his flashlight at the bottom of his duffle bag, left his room, and took the steps down three at the time. He struggled with the side door of the six-car garage, lowered his head against the wind and rain, switched on the flashlight, and followed the singing which grew in volume the closer he came to the cages.

La . . . la . . . laaaaaa . . . la . . . la . . . la . . . la!

Whoever it is, thought Harry charitably though drenched, they got style.

He passed the giraffes and the rhinos and the monkey cages and two timid tapirs and then flashed his light at Llillian, The Llama, who looked at him soulfully. Next the flashlight beam caught Hillard, the ugly gorilla who threw a banana peel at him and missed, and then his beam traveled to the adjoining cage and his chin dropped.

Sitting cross-legged in the cage adjoining Hillard's was a humpbacked blonde Lorelei combing her curls and singing *Caro Nome* in a sweet falsetto to the enthralled lion.

"Vilna! Vilna! Let me in quick! It's *Edna!*"

Vilna sighed with disgust, threw aside her copy of the *Kama-Sutra*, climbed out of bed, threw her robe around her shoulders, crossed to the door, and admitted the wild-eyed woman.

As she shut the door, Vilna trumpeted, "So, if April is the cruelest month, what's already with *June*?"

"Sylvia's *missing!*"

"*Oh.*"

"I just came up and her bed hasnt' been slept in and she said good night over an hour ago!"

"Hmmmm.

"If anything happens to her, Max'll *kill* us."

"Calm yourself, calm yourself, Vilna is thinking. Perhaps she chats with Dylan or the accomodating Gordon or . . . aha!" Mysteriously, she beckoned Edna to follow her. She opened the door and satisfied herself that the coast was clear. Carfully and quietly they made their way to Lord Carson's room. Vilna gently tried the knob and the door opened.

There was no Lord Carson.

Edna had a quick peek over Vilna's shoulder and then led the way back to Vilna's room.

"He has promised to take her exploring, so they have gone *exploring*."

"But where, for crying out loud, in this terrible weather?"

"Beneath the house." Edna's jaw dropped. Vilna smiled smugly. "I myself have had that guided tour by the accomodating unfortunate. If he likes you, he takes you. He liked. He took me. And if you haven't already guessed, the following night he took Max."

"But why didn't they give you a mickey?"

"Because when I went on the tour, there was no shipment. That was Friday night. But Saturday was already a different story."

"Oh my God, supposing there's a shipment down there now? Supposing she and Carson get caught?"

"If she doesn't lose Carson, she will not get caught. He

is very devious and knows his way down there like an emmet in an ant hill."

There was a gentle scratching at the door. Edna leapt for Vilna. "Mice!" Vilna shook herself free with a snort and opened the door. Sylvia flew in.

"Shut it quick!" she whispered.

Edna clamped both fists to her hips. "You got cobwebs in your hair."

Sylvia staggered to a chair and sat. "Oh my God, my god! What I've seen is not to be believed even by the late Robert Ripley. Oh my God, I've got to reach Max. I've got to tell him . . ." she slammed her right fist into the palm of her left hand, "the time to strike is *now*!"

"Discretion, my darling Sylvia," said Vilna like a recently disembodied oracle, "is the better part of valor. Max said tomorrow night . . . and so we wait until tomorrow night."

Sylvia was fighting tears and spoke in a choked voice. "But such human degradation. I've seen nothing like it since my cousin Sophie's wedding. I saw the gypsy girl. Oh my God, she could certainly use a bath. And in an underground cage, I met a certain charming Pandit Perski and, oh my God, he says they've got some kind of system for flooding the place down there and there's this little river that obviously is navigable, straight out to the Thames which is how they get them in and out. And then there's this awful torture chamber and the instruments I saw there I wouldn't wish on my worst enemy, except perhaps my ex-husband Isaac and . . . and . . . ," she sniffled, "not a sign of Quasimodo!"

Vilna's head shot forward like a rooster about to select a hen. "Quasimodoleh? *He's* down there?"

"*Yes*! That's what Lord Carson couldn't remember before! He took poor disguised Quasi down there and *left* him!"

196

Dame Augusta hung up the phone and turned to the others assembled in her private sitting room. Lady Valerie sat on a couch next to Sir Vernon, Judith Sondergaard stood near the fireplace, and Nick Hastings was leaning against the door that connected to the hall.

"Himself has decided. Plan X goes into effect tomorrow night. It will be impossible to unload the shipment soooo . . ." and she shrugged expressively.

Sir Vernon was on his feet. "What about Carson? I won't leave Carson behind."

"Do be reasonable, Vernon. The doctor told you Carson would never survive a trip. He'll be looked after. I've left instructions with my solicitor."

Sir Vernon stood firm. "I won't leave him behind. Have you forgotten what we *owe* him?"

Valerie showed her usual remorse by attacking a cuticle with her teeth. Judith Sondergaard examined her coiffure and Dame Augusta's foot was tapping. Nick Hastings finally broke the silence. "If we take him with us, it's his death warrant."

And Sir Vernon Mayhew went beserk. He leapt across the room and his strong fingers closed around Nick Hastings' neck. Hastings clawed at Sir Vernon's face while Valerie and Judith rushed to the struggling pair and tried to pull Sir Vernon back.

Sir Vernon now had Hastings on the floor, banging his head like a courtroom gavel. "You did it to him! You did it, you bastard! You did it! You destroyed that brilliant brain!"

"Stop that at once!" raged Dame Augusta, "stop that, Vernon, you'll awaken our guests!"

Gypsy Marie Rachmaninoff struggled in the grip of a hideous nightmare. Quasimodo was divesting himself of his disguise when grimy Esmeralda entered the tent. The two youngsters stared at each other with unrestrained passion and there was a background surge of fifty violins scraping away mercilessly at a Brahms Rhapsody. Quasimodo held out his arms and Esmeralda rushed to him, their lips locking passionately.

Then, in the nightmare, Gypsy Marie heard someone say "Jung says transference is the alpha and omega in treatment," and she turned and saw it was Sigmund Freud muttering away as he picked lint from his navel. Then to her added bewilderment she hears Esmeralda say "I'll marry you my hunchbacked beloved because you're a real novelty you are." Gypsy Marie screamed and screamed and heard Quasimodo pleading "Mama! Mama!"

"*Mama, mama, mama!*"

Gypsy Marie struggled awake, her body soaked with perspiration.

"Mama, what's wrong, what's wrong?"

"*Quasi*! My beloved changeling!" She threw her arms around the boy bending over her and smothered his wet face with wetter kisses. Then she cried, "You're soaked to the skin! And goodness your mascara's running. *Where* have you *been*?"

"Brew me a cup of romany tea, mama. And when I tell you where I been, boy, you'll *plotz*!"

Very early the next morning, Detective-Inspector Roberts was awakened by the phone. As he struggled with the bedcovers, he saw and heard the storm outside raging unabated. He spoke into the phone sleepily and heard information that was music to his ears.

"But *how*?" he said in a half whisper and then listened. "You're positive?" and he listened again. His final words before hanging up were, "I'll contact Interpol immediately."

198

Sylvia stared at the phone in the bedroom and wondered if it was too early to call Max. She also wondered if she phoned him would someone listen on an extension. She also wondered how Max would explain a phone call from a lady if he wasn't the first to pick up the phone. She poked Edna and awakened her.

"Damn it, Sylvia, it's not even seven yet!"

"I've been up all night worrying about Quasimodo."

Edna struggled into a sitting position and plumped up two pillows behind her. Then she aimed her mouth at Sylvia and fired. "What's the point in worrying? Vilna finally decided all they can do is lock him up. And if Gypsy Marie was worried, believe me, she'd have stormed the barricades long before this. You look terrible."

"It's still raining cats and dogs. What do we do with ourselves all day?"

"If we know what's good for us, we rehearse some witchcraft. Any ideas?"

"Wait a minute. I brought the handbook with me."

Nick Hastings stood at the bathroom mirror examing the bruises on his neck.

Damn, he thought, I'll have to wear that purple ascot all day and it's for outdoors not indoors. Bloody Vernon. Bloody Carson.

Bloody Carson.

He moved away from the mirror, sat on the toilet bowl with his chin cupped in his hands, deep in evil thought.

Bloody Carson. And bloody Vernon.

Slowly, a malicious smile formed on his lips.

Lovely, he said to himself, oh yes, absolutely lovely.

Dame Augusta strolled with vigorous determination through the covered arcade that connected to the greenhouse. From her left arm there swung a lovely yellow basket, in her right hand, she held a pair of scissors. She entered the greenhouse humming to herself and made her familiar way to the herb garden.

"And how are my pretties this dreadful morning?" she inquired of the herbs and then merrily began snipping away.

Vilna said "Amen," and closed her prayer book to resume chewing over the information Dylan Wake had given her the previous evening. How to transfer this to Max? Must it wait until he arrives this evening with the vicar? Or will it be too late? Dylan, of course, is a misguided wretch, but I adore him and he is my Hamlet and I must see no harm befalls him. True, there will be a bit of a *tsimmis* with Scotland Yard, but surely they will grant him an amnesty and permit him to open at the Old Avon—but of course under police guard. On the other hand, I have undoubtedly some re-casting to worry about. But still, the world unfortunately is filled with actors and all's well that ends well.

Surely they will go easy on Dylan for having turned stool pigeon. But, on the other hand, which of my glorious charms will I have to exercise to make them understand the other slightly embarrassing incident.

The murder.

Amanda Brush volubly cursed the weather from the kitchen window. What will it do tonight? Does it mean moving into the cellar sacrificial room? There isn't the sort of elbow room down there you have outdoors in the garden. But still, she sighed and moved back to the kettle or porridge steaming on the stove, the ladies *are* quite versatile. They'll put on a good show.

"You're talking to yourself again, Amanda," said the vicar as he entered.

"It's the only time I get intelligent answers," she replied testily.

"A bit peevish this morning, are we? Mmmmm, that smells good. Where is our guest? I peeked in his room but it was empty."

"He's having coffee in the study and doing the *Times* crossword puzzle."

Max, seated at the vicar's desk, looked up as the gentle little man entered.

"Good morning! Good morning!" said the vicar cheerfully, "It looks as thogh this dreadful weather will continue all weekend. But still, that won't halt the festivities planned for Astoroth House."

"It'd be a shame if it did," said Max.

The vicar was at the map busily moving pins.

Max said with a smile, "A new plot for Black Bernard?"

"Oh, I've used it before," said the vicar genially, "but this one will have some new variations. By the by, Max, you don't think it will be too much of a shock when you're recognized, do you?"

"No," said Max, "I don't think it will come as a shock at all."

"Don't you think it will put a damper on the festivities?"

"No, Oscar, I don't. I think Astoroth House is always prepared for surprises. Ah!" he said triumphantly as his pencil worked a word into the puzzle, "that's it . . . *Justice!*"

As was their morning ritual, Sir Vernon breakfasted with his son in Lord Carson's room. At the moment, Lord Carson was pouting.

"Why must daddy go bye-bye?"

Sir Vernon fumbled for words. "I have to go away on business."

"But why must mummy and Aunt Augusta go, too?"

"Because . . . because . . . whither I goest, they goest, too."

"Lord Carson come too!" he said firmly.

"You . . . you can't, son . . . you can't. The doctor says travel is bad for your health."

"Who will look after Lord Carson?"

"Good friends. Very good friends. They own a big, white house which is neat and clean and everybody wears white, freshly starched uniforms . . ."

"I won't go there. I *won't*." He pushed his chair back and began stomping about the room.

"Stop that, Carson. You'll make your head hurt."

Carson rushed at Sir Vernon and threw his arms around his father, his face pressed against Sir Vernon's chest, sobbing.

"Oh God," whispered Sir Vernon, "oh God! I can't do it, I can't, I can't do it."

Dylan Wake remained confined to his room with the excuse he was memorizing his lines. He was left undisturbed which soon puzzled and then bothered him. Late that afternoon, with a brave resolve that at first surprised and then filled him with pride, he sat at the writing desk and in two hours filled six sheets of paper which he very carefully hid at the bottom of his suitcase.

The remainder of the household amused themselves with card games, charades, tours of the house and greenhouse, brief rehearsals for the evening's satanic rites. Sylvia Plotkin found it impossible to shake the grim foreboding that had entered her body like a supernatural spirit.

At tea time, the vicar welcomed Channing Roberts and then, at the proper moment, diplomatically excused himself, leaving Max and Roberts to an hour's private and serious discussion.

In Gypsy Marie Rachmaninoff's tent, she was busily arraying herself in a blouse and skirt especially sewn for festive occasions.

"What's with the fancy get-up, ma?" asked Quasimodo as he munched on a chicken leg. "We ain't going anywhere, are we?"

"Oh yes, we are, sweetie," said Gypsy as she applied rouge to her cheeks, "we're going to crash a party."

CHAPTER
fourteen

At about eight o'clock that Saturday evening, a police boat disguised as a pleasure craft came chugging up the Thames towards Punting-on-the-Thames. In the pilot house, the navigator cursed the blinding rain that partially obscured his line of vision. At his left stood a new police recruit wearing a sou'wester and matching hat, and on his right stood Louis Shayne, a colleague of Channing Roberts, wearing a naval captain's uniform and puzzling over a compass in his right hand.

"I still can't figure out the remaining distance to Astoroth House," said Shayne with a scowl, "it's a knotty problem."

"Land ho!" shouted the eager new recruit whose name was Tyrone Powell.

"Tyrone," said Shayne wearily, "if you shout 'Land ho' once more, I'll stuff this compass down your throat."

Tyrone blushed but hadn't the temerity to tell his superior that all his life after a steady diet of sea pictures at the cinema, he'd had this burning ambition to shout "Land ho."

Below decks, a dozen police officers disguised as sailors tugged at the crotches of their ill-fitting trousers and wondered what madness lay before them.

Meanwhile, back in the pilot house, Louis Shayne was cautioning the man at the wheel, "Don't get too close to shore yet. If we run aground, it'll be a dreadful embarrassment."

"Ay ay, sir," said the pilot, who'd read all of Conrad and Melville from cover to cover which was why he was selected for his present assignment."

"Let's hope *their* boat is pulled in at the hidden dock," muttered Shayne, "I don't think they'll see or hear us pull into the adjacent cove, not in this bloody weather." He stared at his compass. "Doesn't this god-damned needle ever point in any direction but north?"

Rom Magyar had been given new heart by Quasimodo's information that Esmeralda, albeit a bit uncomfortable, was still alive and dirty. It was shortly after eight when he sat in Gypsy Marie's tent listening to her careful instructions.

"Keep in mind," Marie cautioned him, "arrive there shortly after midnight. . . ."

Rom Magyar nodded impatiently.

"This is important, Rom Magyar. Everything has been planned down to the last second. Quasi will show you the secret outdoor entrance to the subterranean cellars that Lord Carson took him to. At the appointed moment, you will enter with the selected band of gypsy braves, and for Christ's sake go easy on the tambourines."

Her right wrist shot forward. "Let's synchronize watches."

"Why Dylan darling, you seem your old self again," said Lady Valerie in the actor's bedroom.

"Me old darlin'," he said as he poured himself a third

beer, "my dark cloud has lifted. I feel I'm me old self again."

Truly rotten, thought Lady Valerie, but instead she sipped her Pimms Number Two from a chilled pewter mug.

"The transmigration bit," said Dylan with a lavishly theatrical gesture, "ah, I'm truly in my element with that. I shall give them Edmund Kean."

"Oh charming, charming . . . but don't forget, give them large doses of Jekyll and Hyde mumbo jumbo. You know, lots of writhing and contortion and ugly noises—your usual performance."

"Don't be nasty."

"I'm not. That was meant as a compliment." She walked to him and stroked his cheek. "Dear, dear Dylan, we should have been contemporaries. There might have been a more romantic signature to this chapter in our lives."

He thought about the simulated effort of blinking back a tear, but had already vowed earlier to eliminate all further hypocrisy from his life.

"What's that strange smile?" asked Lady Valerie.

"I was thinking of Max." His head was shaking with wonder. "What a brave bugger he is. You're sure that was him you recognized disguised as a priest at White City?"

"Oh yes . . . quite sure."

Dylan's face hardened. "You're not keeping anything from me, are you, Val?"

"Such as?"

"A plot to murder Max and the ladies?"

"You know I abhor murder."

"You're much too cool about the impending evening. That exterior of yours is more of an iceberg then I've ever seen it before."

"I trust in himself. He says we're perfectly safe. Plan

X is foolproof. The attendants have been thoroughly briefed. They'll cause their diverting diversion . . . and then away we go. But sad—"

"What?" He had the glass at his lips and was staring at her over the rim.

"That the West End will never see your Hamlet."

"I guess it was not in the stars."

Lady Valerie put her hand under his chin and lightly kissed his lips.

"Any last words before we join the others?"

"Yes," said Dylan, "I want you to know this always. You're a great lay."

"Got it down pat?" persisted Edna to Sylvia in their room as a visiting Madame Vilna attacked a fingernail with an emery board.

"Every word and gesture," Sylvia assured her. "But you know something, Edna, I have a feeling we'll never be called upon to do our routine."

"Your mouth to God's ears," intoned Vilna, "it's absolutely *lousy*." She popped the emergy board into her purse and nimbly got to her feet, enjoying the chagrined looks. "But I would not worry if I was you. I think you are right, Sylvia. You will not be called on to say your piece. If, as you told me, Nick Hastings overheard my conversation last evening with my Dylan. . . . "

"Yes?" prodded Sylvia anxiously.

Vilna now seemed transfixed by the storm she was watching out the window.

"That is all I have to say for the moment. I shall join the others now. *A bientot!*" and she swept majestically out of the room.

Edna's head shot around to Sylvia. "And how will *you* behave when Max enters?"

"With decorum," said Sylvia primly, "and I'm watching every bite he takes tonight!"

Vilna left Edna and Sylvia's room in time to see a familiar figure enter Lord Carson's.

"Hmmmm," said Vilna with muted suspicion, and then crossed to Dylan's room and rapped gently on the door. He shouted "Come in," and she went in.

"You have sequestered yourself all day! And why is that?"

"I've been writing something," he said softly as he led her to his suitcase. "It's in there. Everything. Six sheets of paper hidden under my dirty laundry. If anything happens to me, tell Max."

"You *too* have a dark foreboding, eh, me *alte* darling?"

"Face it, Vilna," he said lightly as he swirled the remaining beer in his glass, "I've been living on borrowed time and there's no further borrowing from Peter to pay Paul. Don't look so concerned, me old darlin', I'm not afraid anymore."

"Very brave words, but I look for a symphony, and you give me chamber music. Well then hear this. We were overheard last night by the weasel Hastings."

The blood drained from his face.

Click click click click click.

Needle and wool busily intertwined and Dame Augusta took pride in her amazingly agile fingers.

"Not bad, old girl," she told herself, "not bad for someone your age. No arthritically gnarled digits for you, thanks to my *own* rejuvenation treatments." She paused to think and then looked at the ceiling. "Are you there, Leonard? Are you happy?" She lowered her head slowly. "I hope you are happy, Leonard." Her fingers moved swiftly for another few minutes, and then she held the work up at arm's length.

"Finished. Finished at last. I shall never knit again."

Judith Sondergaard was busy supervising the temporary help in the kitchen when Sir Vernon Hastings entered, looking smart in a tuxedo. Judith flashed him a crooked smile. "I'm preparing Carson's tray. I've doused his trifle with some special brandy.

"There was no need to bother," said Sir Vernon, "I just looked in on him. He's in a very deep sleep."

"Understandable, poor tyke. He's had such an active day."

Vernon rubbed his face with his hands and sighed. "When are they coming for him?"

"Within a few hours if the weather doesn't delay them." She took his hand and said softly, "Dear heart, it *is* for the best."

"I know, I know. But he broke my heart at breakfast. Do you realize Judith. Carson is the end of the Mayhew line."

"But he isn't," whispered Judith.

He looked perplexed. "What do you mean?"

"Oh Vernon," she said with an unbecoming shyness, "can't you guess? I'm *pregnant*!"

He staggered against a table, weakly asked for some brandy, and then wondered why he began dwelling on his instrument case.

Shortly before nine o'clock, the local taxi pulled in at the vicarage and the driver tooted his horn three times.

"Amanda!" shouted the vicar from his bedroom, "tell him we'll be right out!"

Amanda went to the front door and conveyed the message to the driver who then rolled up the window and blew warmth onto his hands as he trembled behind the wheel in his thin jacket.

In the study, Max checked the revolver in his inside breast pocket and concealed it again as the vicar came tripping in carrying an overnight bag.

"Planning to stay the night at Astoroth House?" asked Max somewhat bemused.

"Heavens no!" exclaimed the vicar. "It's my private appurtenances for the orgy. My robe, my wand, and a few other jolly items I bought at a specialty shop in Soho. I must say I admire your calm and reserve. You must be made of steel."

Max crossed to the vicar and picked up his case while Mr. Treble struggled into his raincoat. Amanda was standing in the doorway. "Now, Amanda, you'll be sure to lock up before you leave and of course see to the windows. I'll see you at midnight." Amanda, bristling with unrestrained eagerness, wished them a good dinner and returned to the kitchen. The vicar clucked his tongue as he buttoned up, "Poor Amanda, until witchcraft entered her life, she'd been hiding her light under a bushel. And now comes midnight, it's positively blinding. All buttoned up and ready. Oh Max, you are too kind carrying my bag. Shall I lead the way?"

Trevis Otis, the innkeeper, was speaking into the phone behind his desk in the lobby of the Marksman's Inn. "Ah Miss Sondergaard! Due to the inclement weather, my daughter is a bit indisposed and will be unable to join you this evening. Will you please tell Dame Augusta simply, Miss Otis regrets?" He hung up as Channing Roberts, followed by Willoughby and Simmons, descended the stairs carrying their gun cases. They nodded "good evening" to the somewhat astonished innkeeper as they filed past the desk to the door.

Their gun cases, he thought to himself, at *night* and in *this* weather? I thought mad dogs and Englishmen went out in the noonday sun, but this is certainly an anachronism!

Dame Augusta emerged from the bowels of Astoroth

House into the pantry, made her way to the kitchen where she complimented Judith Sondergaard. "The sacrificial room looks just lovely, dear. Hanging the Mayhew coat of arms over the altar was an inspiration. The underground river looks a bit rough though. I do hope no one slips and falls into it. It's certainly not deep enough for drowning, but there are those crocodiles that escaped this past spring. We can't be too sure where they might be, can we?"

"What time shall I announce dinner?" inquired Judith.

"I should say about half an hour after our guests have assembled. Er. . . ." she looked about making sure they were out of earshot, "the concoction?"

"In the fridge, Dame Augusta, chilling."

"Oh how nice! Dylan does like his drink nicely chilled. Well, Judith, we've come a long way together, haven't we."

"We most certainly have."

"And now we're going a long way. Yes, everything does come to a full circle, doesn't it?"

In a small village of a certain country abroad, and after hours of careful and precise tactical planning, a police force from Interpol invaded and raided a celebrated establishment as per instructions received earlier that morning from Scotland Yard by way of Channing Roberts. Among other enlightening discoveries, in a padded cell they found a teen-age girl going hot and heavy at the typewriter permitted her.

"Wow!" she cried as they burst through her door, "Just the climax I was looking for!" Then her brows furrowed as she inquired, "By the by, what *kept* you?"

The false air of strained conviviality permeating the Crusader Room at Astoroth House was like that of a testimonial dinner in Washington, D.C. attended by a bevy of political rivals. Sylvia traded *bons mots* with a slightly sullen Sir Vernon while a hungry Madame Vilna traded bon bons with Lady Valerie. Edna was displaying a vivacity she usually reserved for a writer's agent she was trying to beat down in a deal, while a startled Nick Hastings heard Dylan Wake whisper in his ear:

"'*Our fancies are more giddy and unfirm.*'" Dylan waved his glass of beer. "Shakespeare. *Twelfth Night.*"

"How clever you are," said Hastings through clenched teeth, while thinking to himself 'Tis a far far better thing that I have done . . . Dickens . . . though slightly revised.

Dame Augusta said, "How unlike the vicar to be this tardy."

Mervyn (in his ill-fitting footman's uniform) entered as though on cue and announced gutterally (having literally been born in a gutter), "The vic-cur and Farther Guh-reen."

Sylvia felt faint and Dylan stepped to her side and put his arm around her waist while clenching his jaws.

Madame Vilna continued grinding a nougat with a cherry center to a pulp while Judith Sondegaard entered quietly from the door that opened into the dining room and positioned herself behind Sir Vernon.

Edna froze and looked like a living statue lacking only the effect of a wreath at her feet.

Nick Hastings fingered his ascot while staring with hatred across the room at Sir Vernon.

Dame Augusta with outstretched hands crossed to greet the vicar as he entered followed by Max Van Larsen.

"Oscar," said Dame Augusta, "you look positively cherubic. And this, of course, is Father Green?"

"If you prefer," said Max with a provocative show of teeth.

"Dear Max," said Lady Valerie coming at him like a guided missile, "I *thought* it was you at White City! But why all the mystery?" She embraced him and Max saw Sylvia blanch.

"I'll explain everything after dinner," said Max, "and I'm sure to everyone's satisfaction."

Dame Augusta said to Max, "*Do* let me mix you a drink!"

Sylvia Plotkin's parting words of assurance the previous night had filled Pandit Perski and his fellow prisoners with a feverish hope for deliverance, but now their ardor was slightly dampened. Pandit poked his friend, one by the name of Ahmet.

"Ahmet."

"Ay?"

"My feet are wet. How's yours?"

"Equally so," said Ahmet, ruefully noticing they were up to their ankles in water.

"Whence comes this?" asked Ahmet nervously.

"From an open cock beneath the floor. Our prayer rugs are ruined."

"Likewise our hopes. What shall we do?"

Pandit Perski clasped his hands together and directed the others. "Let us now yell."

Water! Ugh!

Esmeralda crouched on the cot in her private cell staring at the slowly rising tide.

What evil turn of ·the tide is this, she wondered stupidly.

"Help! Help!" she shouted.

Hank the zoo attendant appeared at the aperture, behind him his associate Tom.

"Let me out," pleaded Esmeralda, "I will drown!"

Hank cackled sadistically.

"My father shall put his curse on you for this! It's no way to treat a Shmeckelecker! What a hideous way for me to die—in water! Oh better the loss of my virginity to this!" She added eagerly, "Any takers?"

At dinner, at least four people were noticeable devoid of appetites, Edna, Sylvia, Max and Dylan. the others ate heartily and with gusto, Madame Vilna twice commending Dame Augusta on the gustatory excellence of the roast boar that had been served.

"Home produced," said Dame Augusta and had she been covered with feathers she might have preened herself.

Max spent the hour and a half fielding questions and jocular innuendo and silently applauded his adversaries for their calm, unruffled, and extremely cocksure miens. *How positive they are of escape. Will there be a slip-up in our strategy?*

Have we been deliberately misled?

Dessert was served and was met with a round of applause for its culinary ingenuity. Dessert was individual ice cream molds of Margaret Hamilton in her role of the Bad Witch in "The Wizard of Oz."

"Copied from an old movie magazine," said Judith Sondergaard gleefully.

After dessert, all moved back to the Crusader Room for coffee and liqueurs and Sir Vernon excused himself, anxious to spend a few last precious moments with Lord Carson.

"Well, Max," said Lady Valerie with an underlined challenge, "how much longer are we to be kept in suspense?"

Max was sharing a love seat with Sylvia and her hand quickly moved and held his tightly. The pressure he returned was loving and reassuring.

"I don't want to spoil the fun you've planned for midnight," said Max.

"You won't be spoiling a thing," said Lady Valerie.

"Everything shall proceed as scheduled, I assure you. Witches rarely alter their timetable. Evelyn, you've been unusually quiet this evening. Joe, you're looking terribly pained. Has dinner disagreed with you?"

"Where's Lisa?" snapped Evelyn.

Lady Valerie was about to speak, but Max intercepted her. "I should say that by now, she is safely ensconced in a very comfortable hotel room."

"Heavens!" cried the vicar, "how do you know that?"

"At approximately ten this evening, a police force from Interpol raided the Swiss Rejuvenation Center. It was a carefully planned surprise party, and since I've received no word to the contrary as pre-arranged, the entire staff must now be in Interpol custody along with Lisa and whomever else they found there. Probably some teen-age girls doped to their ears en route to the Middle and Far East to serve in brothels, and probably some illegal immigrants destined for secret transportation here to Astoroth House."

"Now really!" roared Dame Augusta bravely.

"Do let him finish, Auntie," said Lady Valerie with a Mona Lisa smile.

"At this moment in the subterranean cellar there are at least three imprisoned girls and probably a dozen young Pakistanis and Indians—"

"Two oriyentas," added Sylvia and felt the burning of several pairs of eyes. "Lord Carson took me exploring last night. I saw with my own eyes."

"These illegal immigrants," Max continued almost solemnly, "pay their passage with raw drugs. For example, hash bought in—let us say Lebanon—for about five to fifteen quid a pound is resold here for a thousand and more. Are my figures correct, Joe?"

"Yes," said Gordon, "very correct."

Max turned to Sylvia. "You know *you* were responsible for most of this, don't you?"

"*Me?*" she squealed.

"You started Lisa on her legwork and that clever girl turned her information over to her father who was hoping for a Pulitzer Prize when he broke the story."

"Fat chance," said Evelyn Blair with an unbecoming sneer.

"Unfortunately, Lisa slipped some news to Nelly Locke who in turn told Dylan with whom she was hopelessly in love . . ."

"Very hopelessly," said Dylan staring into his brandy.

"And Dylan like the obedient servant he's been told Lady Valerie and so Lisa was invited for the weekend here. The car bringing her was diverted to the secret boat dock behind Astoroth House and Lisa joined a shipment to Switzerland, by water to Spain and then by private planes to the Rejuvenation Center where the girls are hopelessly hooked on dope and then sent on. Lady Valerie phoned Joe Gordon when she received word Lisa had arrived at the center and blackmailed him into silence. Joe bravely sent for me and that's when our plans for cracking Astoroth House were formulated with Scotland Yard. I assume it was you, Miss Sondergaard, who slipped me the mickey."

"Yes," said Miss Sondergaard drawn up defiantly, "I prepared your cream of mushroom soup with fly ageric we grow in our hothouse here."

The grandfather clock in the hall could be heard beginning to chime midnight.

"Oh dear," said a slightly perturbed Dame Augusta, "the others are undoubtedly gathering in the sacrificial room. We mustn't keep them waiting, you know."

He's got to give himself away soon, Max was thinking, *he's got to!*

Judith Sondergaard caught a subtle signal from someone in the room and quietly exited to the kitchen where she nodded to Mervyn. He dropped the boar's head he'd been gnawing at, put on his raincoat, and went outside.

"What about the murders, Max?" said Evelyn Blair.

"What I have to say about them is pure supposition. But I'm sure in time the people I name will sign confessions. According to Madame Vilna, several people were in a position to poison Leonard Greystoke who tragically learned too much when himself a patient at the Swiss Rejuvenation Center. I'll bet he was costing a pretty penny, Augusta."

"Oh, not all that much, but enough. He forced me to sway the Old Avon board in his favor to play Hamlet . . ."

"Aha!" bellowed Vilna.

"But he was too old and sadly inadequate."

"As I thought," said Vilna to Max, "the poison was in the paper cup pressed to his lips when he collapsed on stage! You, Dylan . . . *you* crumpled the paper cup. I saw it with my own reliable eyes!"

Dylan jumped to his feet. "I didn't do that to him! I didn't!"

Dame Augusta sighed. "Oh sit down, Dylan. Of course you didn't. It was I."

"Auntie!" said Lady Valerie genuinely surprised.

"I always carry a vial of something or other in my knitting bag for emergencies. It's quite painless. I know Irving didn't seem to feel a thing."

"*Auntie!*"

"Well, what the hell," snorted Dame Augusta, "none of *them* is getting out of here alive."

"Max!" Max patted Sylvia's hand but it didn't stop her trembling.

"Nelly," rumbled Evelyn Blair, "who killed Nelly?"

Lady Valerie chimed. "Well, dear Dylan admits he was the last to see her alive."

"Damn bitch!" shouted Dylan.

"Sit down, Dylan," said Max. "I checked Sylvia and Edna as to the time of your arrival at the hotel last night.

Tracing Nelly's movements, she apparently stopped for a drink after leaving you. She was struck on the head by a blunt instrument and traces of blood were found on a statuette in her flat."

"I gave her that statuette," said Dylan glumly.

Max waved him quiet. "By a process of elimination, my candidate for Nelly's murder is *you!*"

Nick Hastings face was as purple as the ascot around his neck.

"Oh *Nicky*," chirruped Lady Valerie, "you went straight from *my* bath tub to Nelly? Good heavens, was that a ritual cleansing?"

"I reserve comment," said Hastings blandly.

"Who stuck that dead bird on our door?" demanded Edna.

"Oh I'll confess to *that*," said Hastings with a smile. "I thought it was a nice touch."

"Extremely macabre," said Sylvia. "If I had my ruler here I'd rap you a good one over the knuckles."

Dame Augusta had arisen. "Well, this has been most entertaining, Max. *Most* entertaining. It'll be a fitting climax to the memoirs I intend writing when I'm comfortably retired in Brazil. But we musn't keep the others waiting any longer. Shall we retire to the sacrificial room?"

CHAPTER
fifteen

Dame Augusta led the way out of the Crusaders Room while Sylvia pulled Max to one side and spoke frantically. "Max, this is insanity! I feel like Alice in Wonderland! They're not the least bit afraid of you. They confess to murder around here like they were playing Twenty Questions! They're so *sure* they're getting away with it!"

"That's right. They're very sure. They have a brilliant plan of escape." He kissed the tip of her nose. "But it ain't gonna work, honey."

"But who's behind all this? Who?"

"That one!"

Sylvia stared at the person leaving the room at that moment and then looked into Max's face with an expression of utter disbelief. "Maxie angel, this is no time for jokes."

"I couldn't be more serious. Or more positive. All I need is proof and I'm trusting to circumstances for *that*. Come on or we'll miss all the fun."

Sir Vernon sat at the edge of Lord Carson's bed and

stared at his sleeping son. Sir Vernon's face was wet as with a handkerchief he wiped the boy's lips of a purple stain.

"Nightshade," he whispered to himself," oh god, how could she . . . how *could* she?"

Then he knelt at the bedside, said a quick prayer, crossed himself, got to his feet, felt the automatic in his inside breast pocket, and mustering the remainder of the courage that had seen him through his public scandal, Sir Vernon marched to the door and opened it.

"Oh dear," said Dame Augusta entering the sacrificial room where Amanda Brush and four other villagers waited impatiently, "what a disappointingly small turn out. Oh well! The inclement weather does play havoc with the box office." She smiled at Amanda. "My robe, dear. Valerie! Judith! Get into your witches' garb!" she smiled at Edna. "My high priestesses. Dylan! Would you step to the altar, dear, just behind the Satanic table. Ah good! The potion is there and waiting. It's nicely chilled, Dylan . . . just the way you like it!"

As she slipped into her robe, she commanded, "Kindly form a semicircle please! Vicar! Would you take your place at the water's edge, please. That's it. Just next to the speed boat! Judith! Start the incantation dear! The kabala, chapter twelve, verse four!"

The gypsies' wagons came up the driveway of Astoroth House.

"I am coming, my Esmeralda!" yodeled Rom Magyar, "soon you shall be reunited with the father who dotes upon your grease-stained head!"

"Around the back" urged Quasimodo, grateful to be out of disguise.

"On the double, men!" urged Captain Shayne as his

men, weapons in hand, clambered over the sides of the boat onto wet land.

Splash.

Shayne walked to the water's edge and said with exaggerated patience. "This way, Tyrone. Land ho."

Harry Sanders made his way with caution through one of the subterranean passages. He reached the cage in which Pandit Perski and friends were about to drown. He unbolted the door, swung it wide, and a torrent of illegal immigrants reached for the rope he lowered to them. When they were safely out of the cage, they followed him to a cell door which he opened and released the two half-drowned girl campers. He then made his way to Esmeralda's cell. He peered through the aperture.

A glum Esmeralda, water up to her neck, said through a cataract of tears. "Just look at me. Look at me. I'm *clean*."

Channing Roberts with Willoughby and Simmons on either side of him belly-crawled through the underbrush towards the rear of Astoroth House.

"Chief!" whispered Simmons through the raging storm, "What's with those animals in the zoo! I've never heard such an uproar!"

Mervyn was rushing from cage to cage releasing the wild animals.

"Transmigration! Transmigration!"

Eyes shut, Dame Augusta was making passes over Dylan Wake's head. Dylan was holding in his hand the poisoned potion.

"Come in, Edmund Kean!" cried Dame Augusta, "come in, Edmund Kean!" she opened her eyes and to Dylan ordered, "Drink it."

Slowly, Dylan lifted the potion to his lips.

On his left, Max felt the movement of a Russian tornado as Vilna suddenly sprinted forward with a shout and slapped the potion from Dylan's hands.

"*Poisoner*!" Dame Augusta recoiled from the flaming-eyed Vilna's accusation.

"You murdering bitch!"

All turned and saw a hysterical Sir Vernon enter brandishing the automatic pointed at Dame Augusta.

"You poisoned Lord Carson!"

"Oh *no*!" shrieked Judith Sondergaard. Lady Valerie's hand flew to her mouth.

"I didn't! I didn't!" insisted Dame Augusta but Vernon's finger had already pulled the trigger. Max leapt at Vernon and caught him around the ankles. Dame Augusta staggered back into Dylan's arms and a familiar voice shouted, "Plan X! *Now*!"

Nick Hastings grabbed Lady Valerie's hand and pulled her towards the waiting speedboat.

A terrified Amanda Brush with the other villagers hot on her heels found the passage that led to the outside at the rear of Astoroth House. She pressed the hidden button. The pintles creaked as the panel swung open and Amanda rushed headlong into a curious hippopotamus.

Roberts and his men saw the hidden panel opening and bravely made their way past the sleepy hippo into the subterranean depths. From around the corner of the house tore Quasimodo, Rom Magyar, and their varied assortment of gypsy henchmen.

At the hidden dock, Shayne and his disguised officers attacked and overpowered the captain and crew of the camouflaged yacht waiting to pick up the escapees from Astoroth House. Then Shayne commandeered a waiting rowboat, ordered eight of his men to accompany him, each positioned at an oar. Shayne yelled, "Pull!"

They pulled.

Shayne raged, "*Forward*, you shmucks! You're rowing us out to sea, damn it!"

Meanwhile back at the zoo, the animals wandered about in complete bewilderment. Only Hillard the Gorilla was enjoying his sudden freedom, swinging from tree branch to tree branch, occasionally pausing to thump his chest and cough as he was out of condition, and finally found the opening that led into the cellars and, with a devil-may-care shrug, entered.

In the sacrificial room, Sylvia wept with despair as the motorboat took off.

"Max! Max!" she cried to her beloved who was still grappling with Sir Vernon, "they're getting away! They're getting away!" Max delivered a powerful uppercut to Sir Vernon's chin and he fell limply to the floor. Harry Sanders arrived with the people he had rescued. From another passageway came Roberts with his two assistants, Quasimodo, Ram Magyar, and company, and then a curious Hillard the Gorilla.

Dylan cradled the dying Dame Augusta in his arms.

"Dear boy," she whispered, "dear, dear boy . . . the best laid plans of mice and men are a crock of cow dung, and quote me."

She expired.

Dylan raised his head and recited slowly:

"*Bear Augusta like a soldier to the stage . .*
For she was likely had she been put on. . . .
To have proved most royal. . . .'

He felt a pat on his shoulder and stared with horror into Hillard the Gorilla's drooling face.

"Urrrrrmph!" said Hillard the Gorilla and Edna nimbly darted for safety.

Esmeralda flung herself into her father's arms and wept.

Judith Sondergaard, who had elected to stay behind

with Sir Vernon, slipped away and rushed upstairs to Lord Carson's room.

Gypsy Marie barred her way.

"I've been waiting for you," said Gypsy with her arms folded. "I'd have been here sooner, but my damn wagon broke down and I had to walk. Well, sweetie, was I right or was I right?"

"Get out of my way," snarled Judith.

Gypsy Marie held her ground and Judith Sondergaard rushed her.

In the sacrificial room, Channing Roberts stood alongside Max at the waterside. They heard the sound of gunfire, shouting, screaming and then soon, the motorboat emerged into view with Captain Shayne standing proudly at the helm.

"Many shots fired!" he shouted, "but not a drop of blood spilled. They're all alive."

The boat pulled in and Shayne leapt ashore.

Splash.

"Oh for crying out loud, Tyrone," he yelled over his shoulder.

"Here he comes," said Roberts to Max as the captives were led ashore.

Max crossed to one person in particular and clamped his hand on his shoulder.

"Sorry, old chap," said Max.

"Tell me this Max, when did you begin to suspect I was behind this organization?"

"When I studied the map in your study with its colored pins. Black Bernard was making too damn many trips."

The vicar sighed.

Gypsy Marie came tearing in shouting, "She's gone mad! Sondergaard's gone mad! She's setting fires all over the house!"

"Everybody out!" shouted Max, "quickly! The place is wired with gelegnitc!"

There was a mad rush for the exits.

Astoroth House went up like a tinderbox and Gypsy Marie cackled. "I told her the house would tremble. I felt the heat in my crystal ball!"

Max and his men had herded everyone to the safety of the front garden with Roberts' men surrounding their prisoners. Dylan stood with Lady Valerie, Sir Vernon, and Nick Hastings. Behind them were the zoo attendants whom several of Shayne's men had rounded up. Edna was within earshot of Valerie and Hastings. She heard Hastings say, "Poor Augusta, she was a brave, valiant woman. Sad she took the bullets meant for me."

Valerie turned a sad face to him. "You poisoned Carson?"

"Yes, my dear. I finally finished the job I set out to do on him two years ago. I always hated him for what he did to my sister. Where is she, Valerie! Where's Mona?"

Valerie shivered in the pelting rain. "She's living with a sheik in the Sahara."

Edna confronted them.

"I overheard," she told them. "Lord Carson was part of this organization?"

"*Part* of it?" cried Valerie. She flung her head back and laughed hysterically as Max, Sylvia, and Madame Vilna joined them. They waited while Valerie's hysterical laughter subsided.

"You fools," she said softly, "you dear poor fools. You especially Max. The real brains was *Lord Carson*."

They could hear the crackling of flames behind them intermingled with a series of muffled explosions.

"Yes, my dears, my brilliant genius of a child, Lord Carson, worked all this out. It was listening to the vicar's stories of the Far East that gave him the idea. Oscar knew where to make the contacts but Carson engineered the plan. The vicar knew all the passages in and out but it was Carson who traveled the east setting up the outlets and making the deals. Unfortunately, he chose to include Nick's sister Mona as one of our victims, he loathed Nick ever since he'd been his fag at Oxford and Nick treated him brutally."

"I was always brutal to my fags," explained Nick, "it was expected."

"*Look*!"

Gypsy Marie was pointing at an upstairs window.

"Look there!"

"Oh, my *God*!" shrieked Sylvia.

In the upstairs window, flames roaring around her like an effigy consigned to an inferno stood Judith Sondergaard. In her arms she cradled the body of Lord Carson.

"She's laughing!" yelled Edna.

"*Judith*!" cried Sir Vernon.

But Judith laughed and laughed and laughed until with a sickening crash, the floor beneath her gave way and she and the dead boy were consumed.

"Mother!" shouted a voice, "Mother, are you all right?"

"I'm over here, Harry darling!"

All gasped as Evelyn Blair ran to Harry Sanders' waiting arms. She kissed him and then turned to her audience. "This is the boy I abandoned for Joseph Gordon, the good son who beat his father over the head with a lead pipe when he mistreated me." She turned to Joe Gordon. "Ironic, isn't it dear? I arranged for his parole board to place him with you, I was so convinced you were a part of this infernal organization."

Max moved to Joe Gordon's side. "He is."

Joe hung his head.

"Joe's madly in love with Lady Valerie, aren't you Joe? You'd do anything for her, and you did. You almost jeopardized Lisa's life."

Joe looked up. "She's not my daughter."

"No," said Evelyn Blair, "she's mine."

"My mind boggles!" That was Vilna.

Evelyn Blair elucidated. "I let Joe and his wife adopt her. I thought they'd give her the home she needed, the one I didn't think I could give her. After all, look at what a mess Harry turned into."

"Ah, ma, I'm reformed now."

"Yes, dear. Mother's very proud of you. And when we're reunited with Lisa, we'll take a nice house in Hampstead and you can both look after me in my old age." She smiled at Sylvia. "Why do you think I showered so much love and affection on Lisa?"

"Mother love," said Sylvia clutching her breast dramatically, "you can't top it!"

"But of course you can!" shouted Vilna, "I was *most* magnificent as the star of *Ess ah Bissel Mehr Zoyerah Kraut Meiner Kinderlach*, which is perhaps more familiar to you as *Mrs. Wiggs Of The Cabbage Patch*!"

Back at the zoo, a contingent of Shayne's men were gingerly rounding up the animals under the supervision of Quasimodo and Harold the Lion who was truly a king of beasts.

The vicar, staring at the smouldering ruins of Astoroth House, clucked his tongue. "Oh dear, oh dear, oh dear. Now I shall never meet the deadline on my next book."

"I don't see why not, Oscar, said Max, "where you're going you'll have loads of time."

The vicar looked at him pixieishly. "Can I have my map back?"

"Max," said Vilna urgently, "I must have a word with you. Concerning Dylan, my stool pigeon."

"Now, Vilna, that little whore steered most of those girls to Astoroth House!"

"Yes, darling, I know. He wrote a complete six-page confession which unfortunately has gone up in flames. But, Max *bubbeleh*, where will I find another Hamlet on such short notice? Isn't it bad enough I have to recast Ophelia and the Player Queen . . . now really, Max, surely we can come to some agreeable aggreement."

Sylvia stepped between them.

"I'm very proud of you, Max. It all worked perfectly. I love you very much, Max."

Max pushed back a lock of her hair, took her face in his hands, and kissed her. Then he embraced her and whispered in her ear, "How'd you like to join me in a little caper in the south of France. Channing Roberts asked me if I'd look into something sinister going on in. . . .

GEORGE BAXT
His Life and Hard Times

On a Monday afternoon, June 11, 1923, George Baxt was born on a kitchen table in Brooklyn.

He was nine when his first published work appeared in the Brooklyn *Times-Union*. He received between two and five dollars for each little story or poem the paper used.

His first play was produced when he was eighteen. It lasted one night.

Mr. Baxt has been a propagandist for Voice of America, a press agent, and an actors' agent. He has written extensively for stage, screen, and television. During stays in England in the fifties and sixties, he wrote a number of films *(Circus of Horrors, Horror Hotel, Burn Witch, Burn)* which are now staples of late night television.

His first novel, A QUEER KIND OF DEATH, was published in 1966. His other novels include SWING LOW, SWEET HARRIET; A PARADE OF COCKEYED CREATURES; TOPSY AND EVIL; "I!" SAID THE DEMON; PROCESS OF ELIMINATION; THE DOROTHY PARKER MURDER CASE; and most recently THE ALFRED HITCHCOCK MURDER CASE.

Mr. Baxt lives in New York, is a bachelor, and is devoted to his VCR.